GRAVE INSIGHT

A MADDIE GRAVES MYSTERY BOOK TWO

LILY HARPER HART

HARPERHART PUBLICATIONS

Copyright © 2015 by Lily Harper Hart

All rights reserved.

No part of this book may be reproduced in any form or by any electronic or mechanical means, including information storage and retrieval systems, without written permission from the author, except for the use of brief quotations in a book review.

❦ Created with Vellum

1. ONE

"It's hotter than Satan's rear end in here."

Maddie Graves glanced up as her grandmother shuffled into her kitschy magic store, aptly named "Magicks," and threw herself into one of the wingback chairs by the front window. Maude Graves started fanning herself with a magazine as she profusely perspired and glared out the window.

"You have a way with words, Granny."

"If you don't stop calling me 'Granny,' I'm going to take you over my knee, Maddie."

"Should I start calling you Maude?" Maddie teased, brushing a strand of blonde hair away from her face and pushing herself up from the floor. She'd been rearranging books and dusting shelves for more than an hour, even though the oppressive heat was pushing her toward the notion of an afternoon nap – or cold shower.

"I prefer Maude to Granny," she said.

"Well, I'll consider it." Maddie exhaled heavily, blowing her damp bangs off of her forehead as she glanced around. "It is hot, especially for this time of year. I can't believe you guys never got central air conditioning in this place."

"It's Michigan, Maddie," Maude said. "You usually get four hot days. It seemed like a waste of money."

"Well, it doesn't seem like a waste of money now, does it?"

Maude shook her head. "Maybe we can go to Traverse City and get some of those window units? The weather forecaster says it's going to stay this way for at least two weeks."

"And we all know how accurate weather forecasters are," Maddie teased. Still, Maude had a point. Living in the old Victorian was like living in a furnace. Heat rises, and while the main floor of the family house had been turned into a magic shop, the upper floors were where they had to live – and try to sleep – every afternoon and evening. It was oppressive up there these days. "I think we should probably go and get a few of them, though," Maddie conceded.

"I want one in my bedroom," Maude said.

Maddie smiled. "I think we should get one for each of our bedrooms, one for the store, and one for the kitchen."

Maude nodded approvingly. "That sounds good. Let's go now."

"It's the middle of the work day," Maddie balked.

"And there's no one out and about," Maude shot back. "People aren't going to a magic store when they have free time. They're going to the lake, or a big mall where there's air conditioning."

The point was hard for Maddie to argue against. She did, though. "It's still not good business practice to post hours of operation and then close early. It's only two hours."

"When you're trying to pretend that your butt isn't sweating and making your girdle all slippery, two hours seems like forever," Maude grumbled.

Maddie barked out a laugh. "Granny ... ."

"I'm just saying ... ."

Maddie shook her head and returned to her organizational endeavor. "It's two hours, Granny. I'll even buy you dinner while we're there."

"Anywhere I want?"

"Anywhere you want," Maddie agreed.

Maude brightened. "I want Ruby Tuesday's."

"I figured you would," Maddie said, smiling. Maude loved the salad bar at the chain restaurant, and Maddie was fairly fond of it herself. Since Maddie had returned to Blackstone Bay, her childhood home, several weeks before, she hadn't had a chance to treat her grandmother to one of her favorite meals. Tonight seemed like as good of a time as any.

Maude studied Maddie for a moment, her face thoughtful. "How are you feeling, Maddie girl?"

Maddie straightened her shoulders and focused on her grandmother. "I'm okay, Granny. I know you've been worried, but I'm okay."

Two weeks before, Maddie had almost died after a run-in with a former classmate and a local teenager. Todd Winthrop and Dustin Bishop had formed an unlikely union, joining together to kidnap and rape women, and then kill them and discard their bodies like trash. Maddie had managed to escape thanks to the intervention of her lifelong best friend, Nick Winters. He'd fought off both men, and then dove into the frigid waters of Willow Lake to retrieve her freezing body and breathe life back into her still lungs.

The night had marked Maddie, and not in the way she expected. Always timid, Maddie now felt a new sense of strength and purpose. She was never going to be one of those women who walked into a room and held everyone's attention on a string as she manipulated them, but she'd vowed to be stronger. She was twenty-eight years old, and she had a lot to be thankful for. Her reforged bond with Nick was only one of them.

"You've been different since that night," Maude said. "You've been … calmer."

"Was I prone to fits of histrionics before?"

"No," Maude said. "You've just been more peaceful. Is it because you saw your mother in the water?"

Maddie's mother had died seven weeks before, an undiagnosed heart ailment cutting her life short while she slept. Since Maddie was psychic and could see ghosts, the death hadn't separated mother and daughter. No, Olivia Graves was still wandering about, popping in from time to time to chat with her only child.

"It's because … I just realized I wanted to live," Maddie said, shrugging. "I realized I want to have a good life. Sitting around and moping is not going to make me happy."

"What is going to make you happy?" Maude probed.

Maddie faltered. "I ... haven't decided yet."

Maude smirked. "Oh, you're such a bad liar."

"What is that supposed to mean?"

"The only thing you need to make yourself happy is about six-feet tall, with dark brown eyes and a killer smile," Maude said. "He's the guy who shows up four times a week to dote on you, and who calls and texts you ten times a day."

Maddie worried her bottom lip with her teeth. "Nick and I are just friends."

"That should be your theme song," Maude said. "You're more than just friends. He sat by your bedside in that hospital for eight hours straight. He held your hand and didn't move a muscle. That's not friendship. It's love."

"Of course we love each other," Maddie said carefully. "We're best friends."

Maude made a disgusted sound in the back of her throat. "I'm seriously going to lock you two up in a room and confiscate all of your clothing. I can't wait much longer."

Maddie rolled her eyes. "You just need to chill," she said. "You're being really pushy lately, and I don't like it."

"That's a grandmother's job," Maude replied, unruffled. "I only have so many years left ahead of me, Maddie. I want to see you happy before I go."

"Oh, Granny, don't say things like that," Maddie chided. "You have a lot of years left ahead of you."

"Of course I do," Maude said. "That's not the point. I want you and Nick settled. This obstinate game you're playing with one another is tiresome."

"It's not a game."

"Oh, whatever," Maude said, getting to her feet wearily. "You ran away for ten years because you didn't want to tell him the truth about your nature. You thought he'd shun you when he found out about your abilities. That didn't happen. He loves you more now than he did when you left – and that's an impressive feat, let me tell you. You just need to suck it up and tell him how you feel."

"He has a girlfriend," Maddie pointed out, her mind briefly traveling to Nick's peaches-and-cream significant other, Cassidy. She hadn't seen the two of them together in weeks, and that had given her hope. She also hadn't heard of their breakup, and that was enough to give her pause.

"Jeepers creepers, Maddie. You are a trip," Maude said. "Fine. Sit in here and enjoy your sauna. I'll be ready at five sharp. I want dinner and air conditioners. You're on notice."

Maddie sighed as she watched her grandmother flounce out of the store. She knew Maude was trying to help. She knew her grandmother had her best interests at heart. She also knew that unrealistic hope, where Nick was concerned, would crush her. So, she'd tamped down her expectations. She'd half-expected Nick to profess his love for her in the hospital when she regained consciousness, but he hadn't. He'd remained by her side for two straight days, making sure she was fed and safe, but he hadn't been romantic.

Maddie was starting to believe the feelings she'd harbored for him were entirely one-sided. Everyone kept telling her one thing, but Nick was still dating Cassidy. There had to be a reason, and that reason was Nick. He genuinely cared about his girlfriend. There could be no other explanation.

Maddie jolted when the bell over the front door of the store jangled, signifying someone was entering. The woman standing there was short, no more than a pixie really. Her brown hair was cut close to her head, offsetting her angular features, and her dark eyes were wide and engaging as they glanced around the store.

Maddie smiled at her. "Hi. I'm Maddie Graves. Are you looking for something specific? I'm sorry about how hot it is in here, by the way. We're going to get air-conditioning units this evening."

"The whole town is on fire," the woman said. "Don't worry. Only a few places in town are cool right now. Why do you think the library is hopping?"

Maddie grinned. "I guess I hadn't thought about that. It makes sense, though."

"I'm Tara Warner," the woman said, extending her hand.

Maddie shook it. "It's nice to meet you. Have you lived in Blackstone Bay long?"

"I moved to the area about three years ago," Tara said. "I work at the flower shop down on Main Street."

"Oh, you work for Mrs. Duncan?"

"She's a wonderful lady," Tara said. "She's getting up there, though, and she just can't work forty hours a week any longer. I love it here, though."

"Did you grow up in the area?"

"I grew up in Charlevoix," Tara explained, referring to another Northern Lower Michigan town. "I used to come over here during the summers, though. I stayed with my aunt."

"Oh, who is that?"

"Chelsea Graham."

"I know Chelsea," Maddie said, smiling. "She's a wonderful lady. Is she still around? I haven't had a chance to see everyone since I got back into town."

"She is," Tara said. "We have tea once a week."

"That's great," Maddie said, shifting. "So, do you need anything specific? Or are you just in the mood to sweat?"

Tara smirked. "I was hoping to get a tarot card reading."

"Oh," Maddie said, surprised. "Sure." She gestured toward the table at the far end of the room. "Have a seat."

Maddie started shuffling the cards when they were settled, holding them out when she was finished so Tara could cut them. Once the woman did, Maddie waited for further instructions. When Tara didn't volunteer them, Maddie chose her words carefully. "Do you have a specific question you want answered?"

"Is that important?" Tara asked, wary.

"Not really," Maddie said. "If you want a general reading, those are easier."

"That sounds good," Tara said. "I used to come in every couple of months and your mother would give me a reading. She was a really wonderful woman."

"She was," Maddie agreed. "I miss her a great deal."

"Still, it's great you opened her shop back up," Tara said. "I'll bet that would have made her proud."

"I'm sure it would have," Maddie said, dealing the cards onto the table. She started the reading, making sure to follow her mother's golden rule: People only want to hear good news. It's not like Tara's cards were full of doom and gloom – that is until Maddie flipped the last card up.

She was so focused on that card – the tower – and it's placement in the spread, that she hadn't heard Tara's question. Maddie shifted her gaze to the woman finally, searching the pretty face for a hint.

"What did you see?" Tara asked, nervous.

"Just that a big change is coming your way," Maddie said, forcing her voice to remain even. There was no way she could tell the woman what she really saw. After all, no one wants to hear about their own death.

2. TWO

"Are you ready to go?" Maude appeared in the doorway that separated the main house from Magicks, impatience flooding her shiny face.

"I'm not sure I can go," Maddie said, her hands clasped on her lap as she stared out the window.

Tara had left about an hour before, her face flushed with excitement (and heat exhaustion), but she'd been happy with the reading. Of course, that was mostly because Maddie had recovered quickly and then proceeded to lie for the better part of an hour. Now Maddie was conflicted.

"What do you mean?" Maude was beside herself. "I want air conditioners."

"I know, but ... there was a woman in here," Maddie said. "She wanted her cards read."

"Well, great," Maude said. "I'll alert the media."

Maddie made a face. "She said her name was Tara Warner."

"The woman who works in the flower shop?"

Maddie nodded.

"What did you see in the cards?" Maude asked, sinking into the chair next to Maddie and sighing. "I'm assuming it wasn't something good."

"She's going to die."

"Well, that's definitely not good. Do you know how?"

Maddie shook her head.

"Well, what are you going to do?" Maude asked.

That was a very good question. "I don't know," Maddie said. "I feel helpless. I can't just blurt it out. People don't like that, and then she'll just freak out and see danger around every corner."

"You could send her an anonymous note," Maude suggested.

"Really? Don't you think that would be weird? What do you want me to do? Should I just write 'you're going to die' on a sheet of paper and slip it under her door?"

"Don't be sarcastic," Maude said. "I'm trying to help."

Maddie sucked in a calming breath. "You're right. I'm sorry."

"You can't just ignore it," Maude said. "If you ignore it, and she really does die, you're going to feel guilty for the rest of your life."

"If I tell her, and she dies, I'm also going to feel guilty," Maddie pointed out. "If I tell her, and she doesn't die, then I'm going to feel like an idiot. I need to think of a better way to approach this."

"I'm sure you could think better if we had air conditioners," Maude said. "And Ruby Tuesday's."

Maddie scrunched her face up as she regarded her grandmother. "We'll go tomorrow. I promise."

"And what are you going to do tonight?"

"Think."

Maude scowled. "You're really not my favorite person right now. You know that, right?"

"I know."

"Good," Maude said. "I'm going to take a cold bath and curse your name. I don't want to see you for the rest of the night."

"Thanks for being supportive," Maddie called to her retreating back.

Maddie returned to her deep thoughts. She needed perspective – and fresh air – to think. She wasn't going to get either in the stifling heat of Magicks – or the frigid cold of Maude's company upstairs. She needed space, and there was only one place to get it.

. . .

NICK WINTERS STROLLED through the woods casually, taking the time to enjoy the darkness as it started to descend. It was still hot and humid, but the sun's retreat offered welcome respite.

He'd stopped by Magicks, hoping to collect Maddie for an evening walk, but a pouty Maude had informed him she had no idea where her granddaughter was. As much as Nick loved Maude, he was glad she wasn't his cross to bear. She was clearly in a mood, and if Nick knew Maddie (which he did) she'd escaped the house with visions of Willow Lake dancing through her pretty head.

Even though the light was waning, Nick never made a misstep. He knew these woods as well as he knew his own yard. He'd spent years frolicking in them with Maddie. They'd built forts under the shaded boughs in the summer, and hunted for mushrooms in the spring. It felt like home.

Nick slowed his pace when he caught sight of the lake, narrowing his eyes so he could scan the beach area. He didn't see Maddie's familiar figure. There was no hint of her honey-colored hair or lithe frame. He was sure she was out here. Now he just needed to find her.

When he got to the edge of the lake, Nick found a familiar pair of Converse discarded on the small beach, as well as a pair of shorts and a tank top. She was swimming. That had to be a good sign. After she'd almost drowned in the lake, Nick had worried she would fear the one place that always offered her solace.

Nick lifted his head and peered into the water. Dusk made his task was difficult, but after a minute, he saw her about fifteen feet out. She was treading water, and her back was to him. Nick grinned as he stripped his shirt off and dropped his shorts on the ground next to hers. He kicked his shoes off and waded into the lake wearing nothing but his boxer shorts.

Nick was purposely quiet as he stroked through the water, closing the distance separating him from Maddie. When he was right behind her, he finally opened his mouth. "It's a nice night for a swim."

Maddie let loose with a blood curdling scream, slapping back at him as she tried to move away.

"It's me," Nick gasped, inadvertently swimming backward. "It's Nick!"

MADDIE FOUGHT to regain her breath, her heart hammering as she tried to calm herself. She had no idea how Nick had managed to get so close to her without sensing his presence. He wasn't a threat, so her inner-danger alarm wouldn't have gone off, but some awareness of her surroundings would have been nice.

"Nicky."

"I'm sorry, Mad," Nick said, instantly contrite. "I didn't mean to scare you. I just ... it was stupid. I'm so sorry."

"It's okay. I just ... I wasn't expecting anyone." Maddie swam in a small circle, collecting herself. "What are you doing out here?"

"I stopped at the house looking for you," Nick said, studying her face. "I thought we could go for a walk. Maude said she had no idea where you were, and she's pissed, by the way. I figured you came down here."

"I ... I just needed some air," Maddie said, swallowing hard. "I'm sorry I screamed at you ... and hit you."

"It's okay, Mad," Nick said, his voice low. "I shouldn't have scared you. After what happened, I ... it was stupid. I'm really sorry."

"I'm okay," Maddie said. "I ... I just wasn't expecting anyone. People rarely come down here during the day. I definitely wasn't expecting anyone after dark."

"Still ... it was a dumb move."

"It's okay," Maddie said, gracing him with a genuine smile. Her heart was slowly returning to a normal beat. "How was your day?"

"Hot," Nick said. "How was yours?"

"The same."

"Why is Maude upset?"

"I promised her we would go to Traverse City and buy some air conditioners," Maddie said. "Then I got ... sidetracked."

"With what?"

Maddie stilled, unsure how to answer. Nick was aware of her "peculiarity" now. He knew she was psychic and could talk to ghosts. She was still nervous about talking to him when it came to her abilities. "A woman came in the shop today to have her cards read," Maddie said. She'd promised Nick nothing but the truth from here on out, and she was determined to keep her word. "It wasn't good."

"Who was it?" Nick asked, not missing a beat.

"Tara Warner. Do you know her?"

Nick wracked his brain. "Is she the woman who works in the flower shop?"

"Yes."

"What's going to happen to her?"

"She's going to die," Maddie said, her voice small.

"Do you know when?"

"No."

"Do you know how?"

"No."

"Okay," Nick said, resolute. "We'll figure something out. You can't save everyone, Mad. We can only do what we can do. I'll try to see what I can find out about Tara and who she hangs around with."

"How are you going to do that?"

"I'll go in and buy some flowers. You know, just talk to her," Nick said. "I'm a trained officer. I'm good at my job."

"I'm sure you are," Maddie said, smiling. "You're good at everything you do."

"And don't you forget it," Nick said, stroking closer.

Nick's proximity made Maddie aware of her current predicament. She'd come down to the lake to dip her toes in the water, not go swimming. The water had felt so nice, though, she'd risked wading into it. She'd been briefly worried it would still be cold enough to remind her of the worst night of her life. Instead of cold, though, Maddie only felt refreshed. Since she was alone, she'd stripped out of her clothing and dove in. She hadn't been wearing a bathing suit under her clothes, and she hadn't wanted to ruin her expensive bra and panties, so she'd entered the water bare of anything but her smile.

There was no way Nick could know that, and Maddie was positive she'd die of shame if he found out. She had no idea how she was going to get out of the water with her modesty intact.

NICK WAS RELIEVED to find Maddie relaxing. Somewhat. She wasn't terrified anymore, but there was something else going on. He reached out to her instinctively, his fingers brushing against her bare midriff.

"Aren't you going to give me a hug?"

Maddie balked. "What?"

"You always give me a hug," Nick teased. "I haven't had my daily dose of Maddie yet."

"I ... I can't."

Nick furrowed his brow. "Why?"

"Because I'm swimming," Maddie replied primly. "I need my arms to stay above water."

"I'll hold you up." Nick swam closer. "Come on. Give me a hug." He reached for her, and when Maddie moved to swim away, Nick grew concerned. "I'm sorry I scared you."

"It's not that," Maddie said, glancing around helplessly. "It's just that ... ."

"Mad, you're starting to scare me," Nick said. "Why won't you let me touch you?"

"I ... I can't tell you. You'll never let me live it down."

Nick was confused. His gaze bounced between Maddie and the shore she was longingly staring at, and then realization dawned. "Are you naked?"

"What? No!"

"You are, aren't you?" Nick was intrigued. Maddie clothed was a sight to behold. Maddie naked could be nothing short of breathtaking.

"I ... I thought I was alone," Maddie admitted, miserable. "I didn't think anyone would see."

"I haven't seen anything," Nick reminded her. *I just want to.* "I promise to be a gentleman if you give me a hug."

"No," Maddie said, scandalized. "You'll ... feel everything."

"You know I've felt that before, right?"

Maddie frowned. "How many women have you brought down here to go skinny dipping?"

"None. That's not what I meant. I just meant you don't have any parts that would mystify me," Nick said. "I ... if you don't want to give me a hug, you don't have to. Just know, you're really hurting my feelings."

He was messing with her, but he wanted to see how she would react.

"You don't play fair," Maddie said, chewing on her bottom lip.

"You want this to be fair?" Nick challenged.

Maddie nodded.

Nick reached under the water and tugged his boxer shorts off, holding them up so she could see them, and then tossing them toward the shore. He had no idea if he would find them again, and he was beyond caring. He was much more interested in finding out what Maddie would do next. "Now we're both naked."

"Oh ... my ... oh."

Nick grinned. "Now give me a hug."

Maddie swam toward him, still uncertain. Nick had to fight the urge to kiss her the minute he felt her skin touch his. Instead, he kept his breathing even and wrapped his arms around her back, relishing the feeling of her body as she pressed in closer. He almost lost himself when he felt her breasts, the nipples erect, press against his chest. Nothing had ever felt this right.

Nick purposely shifted his lower body so Maddie couldn't feel the excitement pooling in his groin. She definitely wasn't ready for that. Nick held her for a full minute, breathing in deeply as she rested her head against his shoulder.

"See, that wasn't so bad," Nick said when he finally released her. Maddie moved away, but only marginally. He could still feel her warmth when she looked up at him. "Nothing bad happened. You were perfectly safe."

"I'm always safe with you," Maddie said, her breathing ragged for an entirely different reason than a few minutes before.

"You are," Nick agreed. Her lips were right there. He could taste her. Finally. She would let him. They could be together.

Maddie increased the distance between them slightly. "So, how is your girlfriend?"

Nick scowled. He really needed to take care of that situation.

3. THREE

Maddie's question was pointed enough to kill the mood.

Nick cleared his throat, uncomfortable with the way her blue eyes were searching his face. He knew she'd been excited to be in his arms. Her flesh had quivered when they touched. That was why she was asking about Cassidy now. She was trying to create distance between them. She wasn't the kind of woman who moved in on someone else's turf.

"Mad... ."

"No, it's fine," Maddie said, pointing herself in the direction of the shore. "It's none of my business."

Crap. This situation was getting out of hand. "Maddie, we need to have a talk."

"It's fine," Maddie said. She was farther away now, almost to the shore. "Turn around until I'm dressed."

That was the last thing Nick wanted, but he obliged. After a few minutes of facing the opposite shore, Maddie spoke again. "Okay, you can come out. I'll turn around until you get dressed."

"Great," Nick said, his tone dull.

He didn't bother to look for his boxer shorts. When he was dressed, he crossed his arms over his chest and watched Maddie for a moment. Her blonde hair was damp and hanging down her back, and she was steadfastly refusing to even peek in his direction. It was kind of cute. Oh, who was he kidding, it was outright adorable.

"You can turn around," Nick said. "Your virtue is perfectly safe."

Maddie's face was unreadable when she faced him. "Did you find your boxers?"

"I think I sacrificed them to the lake gods," Nick teased. "They died a good death."

Maddie couldn't help but giggle. "Funny."

"I try."

Nick gestured to the sandy beach. "Why don't you sit with me? There's nothing but a hot house and an even hotter Maude waiting for you at home. At least it's comfortable out here."

The duo settled onto the beach, shoulders touching. There was still an unspoken wedge between them, and it revolved around Cassidy. Nick didn't want anything between them. He just had to take it one step at a time. He couldn't make a move on Maddie – at least not yet.

"I'm breaking up with Cassidy," Nick announced. Maddie's face was blank, so Nick plowed on. "I've been planning it for some time, but ... I hate being the bad guy."

Maddie pursed her lips. "It's really not any of my business."

Nick sighed, running his hand through his dark hair. "You're my best friend, right?"

"Of course."

"Don't best friends sit and listen when people complain about their romantic problems?"

Maddie's face softened. "You're right. Why are you going to break up with Cassidy?"

"I was going to break up with her before you even came back," Nick said. "I just got ... distracted."

"With me?"

Nick smiled. "Amongst other things."

"Christy says you have a six-month cycle," Maddie said carefully. "You date a woman for six months and then end it like clockwork. Is that true?"

"Yup."

"Doesn't it bother you that everyone knows about your cycle?"

"Nope."

"Really?" Maddie seemed surprised.

"Really," Nick said. "I figure, if people know about the cycle, they won't be offended when the end comes. They're less likely to take it personally when everyone in town already knows it's true. The problem is, even though everyone told her about the cycle, Cassidy is refusing to see the writing on the wall."

"So, tell her."

"I usually prefer it when they break up with me," Nick said. "In the past, I've just distanced myself and they've gotten the hint and dumped me. I like it that way."

"You never could handle being the villain," Maddie said, laughing. "When we played as kids, you always had to be the cop and not the robber."

"I'm fond of my white hat."

"I don't pretend to understand your relationship with Cassidy," Maddie said, cautiously choosing her words. "If you're not happy, though, you should do what makes you feel better."

Nick smiled internally. She was trying to hide her excitement, but he could feel it positively rolling off of her. She was entrenched in "friend" mode, but she was ready to climb a new rung on their relationship ladder. The realization made him indescribably giddy. He tempered his enthusiasm. "She knows I'm not in love with her," he said. "She just refuses to accept it. She wants to go to couples' counseling."

Maddie snickered. "Really?"

"She told me the night Todd went after you," Nick said. "She was in my office, and I was going to do it then, but Maude came running in and ... well ... there was a damsel in distress who needed me." Nick winked at Maddie, charming her to the tips of her toes.

"That was two weeks ago," Maddie pointed out.

"I know," Nick said. "I haven't had a chance to pick up where we left off."

"She hasn't called you in two weeks?" Maddie was doubtful.

"Oh, she's called. I just haven't answered."

"You've been dodging her calls for two weeks? Nicky, that's horrible."

"I know," Nick said. "I just ... I can't break up with her over the phone, and I really don't want to do it in a public setting."

"So, take her out to dinner, be polite, and then do it on the ride home." Maddie was warming to the topic.

Nick grinned. "Yeah, that will be a fun ride."

Maddie sighed. "Sorry. You're right. You have to do it in your own way."

"I do," Nick said. "I just need to figure out how to do it without crushing her."

"I'm not sure if that's possible, Nicky," Maddie said. "She's very much in love with you."

"You've been around her twice," Nick pointed out. "How do you know that?"

"You can just tell when someone loves someone," Maddie said simply. "It's written all over their face."

"You can indeed," Nick said, studying Maddie's beautiful cheekbones. "You can indeed."

"WHERE HAVE YOU BEEN?" Maude asked.

She was sitting at the kitchen table, a glass of iced tea and a flask of bourbon in front of her, when Maddie returned to the house.

"I went swimming down at the lake."

Maude straightened in her chair. "By yourself? Was that smart?"

"It was fine," Maddie said, sitting in one of the open chairs. "I was in no danger." *From anything other than losing my heart*, she added silently.

"You were gone a long time," Maude said. "I was starting to get worried."

"Nick showed up, and we talked for a little bit."

Maude smiled. "Did he swim, too?"

"Yes."

"Were you naked?"

"Who told you that?" Maddie's eyebrows flew up her forehead.

Maude cackled loudly. "You just did. Wow. Did you two ... ?"

"Of course not," Maddie said. "He has a girlfriend. It was ... innocent."

"Oh, sure. One hot boy, plus one beautiful girl, plus no clothes ... yeah, that usually equals innocence."

"We just talked," Maddie said. *And hugged. Oh, God had they hugged.*

"What did you talk about?" Maude asked.

"If I tell you, you have to promise not to tell anyone else," Maddie cautioned.

Maude leaned forward, practically drooling with anticipation. "I promise."

"Nick says he's going to break up with Cassidy."

Maude's reaction was blasé. "Of course he's going to break up with Cassidy," she said. "That was never in doubt. What else did he say?"

"Just that he's been trying to do it for weeks," Maddie said, taken aback. "I thought you would be excited."

"Why would I be excited about that?"

"Well ... ." Maddie wasn't sure what to say. "I just thought ... I don't know. Forget it."

"You're so darned adorable I can't stand it sometimes," Maude said. "Nick told you that he's going to break up with his girlfriend, and now you're starting to wonder if he has feelings for you. You can't wait for Cassidy to get the heave-ho because you want to see what Nick will do.

"News flash, Maddie girl, Cassidy was never standing in your way," she continued. "Nick was never torn between the two of you. He just doesn't want to hurt Cassidy. He's a good guy, but he's a wuss when it comes to things like this."

"I ... well, what do you think he'll do once he breaks up with her?" Maddie was being coy.

"I think he's going to make a beeline here so he can kiss you senseless."

Maddie exhaled heavily. *What would that be like?*

"I still think he's going to have to get up some courage to cut Cassidy's knees out from under her," Maude said. "You're going to have to be patient."

"I'm patient."

"Of course you are," Maude said, patting her hand. "You've been waiting for him for eleven years. A couple more days aren't going to kill you."

Maddie shook her head, fighting the urge to smile, but ultimately losing. "You're loving this, aren't you?"

"I love you, Maddie girl," Maude said. "I love Nick, too. The boy has always been loyal, and funny. And let's face it, he grew up to be a real looker. I want you to be happy."

"But?"

"But he's not going to dump Cassidy right this second," Maude said. "He's too much of a gentleman to swim naked with you and then drive straight over to her house and dump her. He's going to have to buy her dinner first."

"That's what I told him to do," Maddie said, surprised.

Maude giggled. "Great minds."

"Well, speaking of dinner, I promise to take you out for a nice one tomorrow," Maddie said. "In fact, why don't we leave early in the afternoon? I'm running over to the salon to see Christy in the morning, but we can leave right after lunch to go to Traverse City."

"What about the store?"

"It's too hot for anyone to come into the store," Maddie said. "Once we get the air conditioners, more people will be willing to brave the shop."

"Why are you going to the salon?"

"Um ... I just want to get my hair trimmed up a little bit," Maddie replied evasively.

"You mean you want to make sure you're looking good for when Nick comes calling," Maude supplied.

"That is not true," Maddie protested.

"Oh, whatever," Maude said. "You just got your hair trimmed two weeks ago."

"Fine. I don't have to go to the salon. We can leave first thing in the morning."

"No, you're going to the salon," Maude said.

Maddie arched an eyebrow. "Are you sure?"

"Make sure you get your eyebrows waxed while you're there," Maude said. "You need to look perfect when destiny comes knocking."

Maddie stuck her tongue out at her grandmother.

"Brush your teeth, too," Maude said, ignoring the gesture. "Use a lot of mouthwash. You don't get a second chance to do a first kiss the right way."

"Thank you, Granny," Maddie said.

"Oh, and shave your legs."

"Okay." Maddie snatched the bottle of bourbon from the table. "You're done with this for the night."

Maude blew an unladylike raspberry in Maddie's direction. "You might want to buy some cuter underwear, too."

Can people die of embarrassment? Maddie was worried she was about to find out. "I'm going to bed."

"Sweet dreams," Maude chortled. "Or, in your case, naughty dreams."

"Granny!"

4. FOUR

"**W**ell, girl, you are a sight for sore eyes."

Christy Ford was five feet and five inches of enthusiasm wrapped in a busty red-headed package. When she caught sight of Maddie slipping through the front door of her salon the next morning, she was on the willowy blonde and welcoming her with a warm hug before Maddie could even catch a breath.

"It's good to see you," Maddie said, laughing despite herself.

When they'd been in high school together a decade before, Christy had been one of the few girls Maddie had gotten along with. Most of the others were minions of Marla Proctor, Blackstone Bay's resident mean girl, and Marla hated Maddie with a passion. Marla enjoyed torturing weaker girls, and Maddie and Christy both fell into that category as teenagers. While Maddie and Christy hadn't been close friends, they had never been enemies either. Once Maddie returned to Blackstone Bay, Christy had turned her into a pet project, and the two had struck up a fast friendship.

Maddie was genuinely fond of the woman, and she was forever thankful for the friendship she'd been offered without question or reserve.

"Come and sit down," Christy said, gesturing to her station.

Christy was the owner of Cuts & Curls, buying it from the former proprietor a few years before. It was Blackstone Bay's only salon, and with that, Christy had a certain amount of power and standing in town. She loved lording it over people, too. "What are you here for?"

"Just a trim," Maddie said.

"Didn't you just get a trim a few weeks ago?"

"I ... yeah," Maddie said. "The ends are just a little ragged, though. Oh, and Maude says I need to get my eyebrows done."

Christy snickered. "No problem." She draped a frock over Maddie to protect her clothing. "So, how are you feeling?"

"I'm fine."

"You almost died," Christy said. "If Nick hadn't found you ... ." She broke off, glancing over her shoulder quickly before lowering her mouth to Maddie's ear. "Cassidy is in the back. Be careful."

Maddie froze. The last thing she wanted to do was run into Nick's girlfriend. "Maybe I should come back later."

Christy shook her head. "No. That will just make her suspicious."

"What does she have to be suspicious about?" Maddie squeaked.

Christy shot her a knowing look in the mirror. "Who do you think you're trying to fool?"

Christy had been pushing Maddie in Nick's direction with the same amount of force Maude had been simultaneously shoving her. Christy was convinced Nick and Maddie were soul mates, and she'd made her opinion on Cassidy's future pretty obvious.

"I ... ."

"Just sit there and let me cut your hair," Christy ordered. "Tell me what the latest is on Todd Winthrop."

Maddie scowled. In addition to being a murderer, Todd had also been a local celebrity. His arrest was still the cream of the gossip crop in Blackstone Bay. The fact that he'd enlisted a high school standout to help him with his murderous plans only made things that much more titillating.

"He's being held in the county jail," Maddie said. "He says he's being framed, but they found a lot of evidence in Dustin's house, and

Dustin is trying to get a deal so he's been telling the cops everything. Nick says it's open and shut."

"That's good," Christy said, fluffing the top of Maddie's hair. "Are you having nightmares?"

"I did the first few nights," Maddie admitted. "I haven't had one in more than a week, though."

"That's good, right?"

"It is."

"How have you guys been dealing with the heat?" Christy asked.

"Not well," Maddie said. "Maude is about to have a meltdown. We're going to Traverse City this afternoon. I'm buying her dinner and air conditioners."

"Well, that sounds fun," Christy said, smiling.

"Then I'm telling it wrong."

"How are ... other things?" Christy asked, scanning the space behind her to make sure no one was eavesdropping. Cassidy's eyes were trained on them, but she was too far away to hear the chatter.

"Do you know Tara Warner?"

"The woman from the flower shop? Yeah. She comes in every few weeks for a cut. Why?"

Maddie told Christy about Tara's bleak reading, being careful to keep her voice low and the story short. "What do you think?"

"I think I see another adventure in our future," Christy teased.

"Absolutely not," Maddie said, shaking her head.

"Hold your head still," Christy ordered. "Do you want me to cut all of your hair off?"

Maddie instantly stilled. "We are not going on another adventure."

"We'll see," Christy teased. "I'll see what I can find out about Tara, though. She's pretty quiet. I've never heard of anyone having a problem with her."

"That's what makes me nervous," Maddie said. "If no one has a motive, how do you shrink the list of suspects?"

"Well, I think we can cross Todd off the list."

"Thank the lord for small favors," Maddie murmured.

The bell over the front door of the salon jangled, and Christy and Maddie lifted their eyes in unison. The look on Christy's face was murderous when she recognized the woman standing in front of the counter.

Marla Proctor was a beautiful specimen of the female form. She was rail thin, with petite bone structure and long legs. She was also nasty and mean, which made her outside ugly by virtue of proximity to her toxic insides.

"Marla, you've been banned," Christy said.

"Oh, Christy, don't be like that," Marla said, her voice pleasant. "We had a misunderstanding."

"It wasn't a misunderstanding," Christy replied. "I'm not putting up with your crap. I told you when I took this place over that I wouldn't allow you to trash talk my clients. You did. You're not welcome here anymore."

What Christy wasn't saying out loud – mostly because she didn't want to embarrass Maddie – was that the client Marla insisted on torturing was the blonde sitting in the chair in front of her.

"Come on, Christy," Marla pleaded. "I have a date tonight. I promise I'll be good. I'll never say a bad thing about any of your clients again."

Christy made a face, and an exasperated sound in the base of her throat. Everyone in the salon knew that was an empty promise. "If you say one bad thing ... ."

"I won't," Marla said, raising her hand.

"Fine," Christy said. "You have to wait your turn. I'll get to you when I'm done with Maddie."

Marla shot Maddie a harsh look, opening her mouth to say something tart, but snapping it shut when Christy glanced in her direction. "I'd love to wait."

"Great," Christy said. "Who is your big date with?"

"His name is Charles Hawthorne," Marla said, her eyes sparkling. "He's a third."

"A third of what?"

"No, he's the third in his family with that name. They're all rich investment bankers."

Christy wrinkled her nose. "I've always heard that people with numerals after their names are horrible in bed."

Maddie couldn't stop herself from laughing, the sound escaping her mouth before she could haul it back in.

Marla narrowed her eyes. "I think that's an urban myth."

"Well, you'll have to keep me updated," Christy said. "Okay, Maddie, your hair is done. I'll get the wax for your eyebrows." Christy paused next to Marla. "If you say one nasty thing to her, I'll shave your head bald."

Marla was affronted. "I said I'd be good."

"Yes, but I'm leaving the room for a second, and I have my doubts about whether you'll be able to rein yourself in," Christy said. "Just know, I'll be taking a poll when I get back. If one person in this salon thinks you were being mean in my absence, you're out."

"I said I would be good," Marla protested.

"You'd better be."

Once Christy disappeared into the back room, Maddie was uncomfortable with Marla's studied gaze. If history was any indication, being this close to Marla would be detrimental to Maddie's emotional wellbeing.

"So, how are you, Maddie?" Marla asked stiffly.

"I'm fine. Thank you for asking."

"I was sorry to hear about what happened to you," Marla said. "I always knew Todd was a little ... out there ... but I had no idea he was capable of the things he did. It's a miracle you survived."

"I was very lucky," Maddie agreed.

"You were lucky that Nick saved you," Marla corrected. "He fought two healthy men and beat them both, and then he dove into freezing cold water so he could drag you back to shore."

"He's a good friend," Maddie said evasively.

"Yes. *Friend*."

"I hope your date goes well," Maddie said, desperately trying to change the subject. The last thing she needed was for Cassidy to be drawn into the conversation.

"Oh, it will," Marla said. "I bought a new dress and some great new underwear."

Maddie wasn't sure how to respond to that. "Oh, well ... good."

"It will be good," Marla agreed.

Christy moved back behind Maddie, her eyes suspicious as she surveyed the scene. "And how are things?"

"They're fine," Marla said. "I was extremely pleasant."

Christy looked to Maddie for confirmation. "We had a nice chat," Maddie said.

"Good," Christy said. "Give me a few minutes, Marla. Maddie's eyebrows are practically perfect as it is. It will only take me a few minutes to touch them up."

"Sure," Marla said, lowering her chin. "I will wait quietly and with respect."

Christy rolled her eyes. "And in those chairs out there." She pointed to the front of the salon. "I don't need you crowding us."

"Fine."

Once Marla was gone, Christy and Maddie avoided eye contact in the mirror. They both were afraid they were going to burst out laughing.

"So, other than an afternoon with Maude, what are you doing tonight?"

"Not much," Maddie said. "The only thing I care about is getting those air-conditioning units in the windows. It's been too hot to sleep for three nights. I actually had to go down to the lake to cool off last night."

"Oh, wow," Christy said. "Was that the first time you went back?"

"No. It was the first time I got into the water, though."

"That's pretty brave," Christy said.

"When you're sweating to death, bravery is a state of mind."

Christy giggled, shifting as a figure approached her from behind. "Oh, hey, Cassidy. Do you need something?"

Cassidy's strawberry-blonde hair was freshly washed and curled, and her face was unreadable as she studied Maddie. "No. I just wanted to tell Maddie how relieved I am that she wasn't hurt."

"Thank you," Maddie said.

"Nick was beside himself," Cassidy said. "In fact, ever since that night, he's been kind of hard to get in touch with."

"I ... ."

"You should probably talk to Nick about that," Christy said, cutting Maddie off.

"Oh, I plan to," Cassidy said. "In fact, he's taking me out to a romantic dinner tonight. We're going to talk about everything and get our relationship back on track. Now that Maddie isn't in imminent danger, it seems I have a chance to reclaim my boyfriend."

Maddie swallowed hard. "Good for you."

"Yes, good for you," Christy said. "You can just leave the money on the counter. I'll pick it up when I'm done with Maddie."

Cassidy seemed surprised by the dismissal. "I ... I didn't mean anything."

"It's fine," Christy said breezily. "Just put your money on the counter and enjoy your date."

Cassidy straightened, smoothing the front of her flowery peasant blouse down as she tried to regain control of the situation. "I will enjoy my date. It's going to be a great night."

"I'm sure it will be," Christy said, focusing on Maddie's eyebrows. "Stop wrinkling your forehead, Maddie."

"It's going to be a great date," Cassidy repeated.

"Good," Christy said.

With nothing left to say, and clearly not garnering the reaction she'd hoped for, Cassidy had nothing left to do but retreat. She shuffled to the front desk, dropped her money on the counter, and then disappeared through the front door. She cast one more dark look in Maddie's direction before moving away from the salon.

Christy waited exactly one minute before asking the obvious question. "So, Nick is going to break up with Cassidy tonight, huh?"

Maddie was flabbergasted. "How did you know that?"

"He's been dodging her for two weeks," Christy replied. "Helen

Marks said that she saw them both in the grocery store at the same time, and when Nick realized Cassidy was there, he actually dropped to his knees to hide behind the apple stand."

"I ... I don't know for a fact that he's going to break up with her tonight," Maddie cautioned.

"Oh, well, that was convincing," Christy teased.

"I don't know."

"You're a funny girl, Maddie Graves," Christy said, gripping the edge of the paper strip and ripping it away from Maddie's forehead quickly. "A funny, funny girl."

Despite herself, despite the admonishments she'd been giving herself for weeks, Maddie was filled with sudden hope. Was Nick officially going to be on the market in a few hours?

"Hurry up," Maddie said. "I want to get over to Traverse City and back as soon as possible."

Christy grinned. "Yes, ma'am."

5. FIVE

"I ... we're eating here?"

Nick didn't miss the look of disappointment as it washed over Cassidy's face. "Is that a problem?"

When he'd finally gotten up the courage to call Cassidy earlier in the day, he'd been expecting an explosion of anger and recrimination. Instead, Cassidy had been ... pleasant. No, she'd been beyond pleasant. She'd been sweet, nice, and conciliatory. That bothered Nick more than a verbal beat down ever would.

"No. It's fine," Cassidy said, forcing her face to remain neutral. "I just thought we would go somewhere more ... romantic. Ruby Tuesday's, though. I ... they have a great salad bar."

Nick swallowed his internal sigh. He'd purposely picked a chain restaurant because he didn't want to give Cassidy unrealistic expectations. He wasn't going to sit through a tense dinner. He was going to try and explain his actions. And then, when they were close to Blackstone Bay, he was going to drop the hammer on her. He was genuinely sorry because he knew she was going to be hurt. He couldn't put his happiness on hold any longer, though. He wanted Maddie. He'd always wanted Maddie. Cassidy was just going to have to accept that they were never meant to be.

"I love the salad bar," Nick said. "They have great steak, too."

"Well ... good," Cassidy said.

They were standing in the lobby and waiting for the hostess to return. The restaurant was busy, but the hostess had promised the wait wouldn't be too long.

"So, how has work been?" Cassidy asked.

"Busy," Nick said. "We're still gathering evidence on Winthrop and Bishop, and the prosecutor is going to be in the office tomorrow for a final meeting."

"That's good, right?" Cassidy asked, hopeful. "That means your schedule should lighten up."

"Maybe," Nick said evasively. "We also have the big fair coming up, and we have to coordinate for that."

Cassidy ignored the comment. "And now that Maddie is perfectly fine, she won't need you hovering every day."

Nick swallowed. "I haven't been hovering."

"You slept in a chair next to her bed in the hospital, even though I was waiting in the lobby all night," she pointed out. "You spent the first two nights after she returned sleeping on her couch." The unspoken accusation left hanging in the air was that Nick had slept elsewhere – like Maddie's bed. He didn't bother to acknowledge it.

"She almost died," Nick said.

"And I'm sure she used that to her advantage," Cassidy mumbled.

Nick frowned. "That's not who Maddie is."

"Oh, right," Cassidy said. "Maddie is too sweet to use her near-death experience to tug at your heartstrings. I forgot."

The more she talked, the more Nick wanted to choke her with a hard dose of reality. He refrained, though. He knew she was going to freak out, and he didn't want it to happen in a busy restaurant. "I would appreciate it if you didn't say nasty things about Maddie."

"What was nasty? It was the truth."

"Your truth," Nick said. "Your truth is different from my truth."

"And what's your truth?" Cassidy challenged.

"My truth is that Maddie was stalked through the woods and almost killed. My truth is that Maddie almost drowned. My truth is not that she needed me, but that I needed to be there for her. That's my truth."

Cassidy shrank in the shadow of Nick's harsh words. "I ... I didn't mean to say anything bad about your precious Maddie."

"Good," Nick said, focusing back on the hostess stand. "Good grief. How hard is it to find out if a table is open?"

The sound of familiar bickering assailed his ears as the front door of the restaurant opened behind him.

"I'm not saying I'm embarrassed," Maddie said. "I'm saying that the boy who helped us load those air conditioners into the truck didn't look happy when you told him he had a nice butt."

Nick couldn't help but smile, an expression that wasn't lost on Cassidy as her gaze bounced between her boyfriend and his best friend.

"He did have a nice butt," Maude said. "It was one of those round ones you just want to squeeze." Maude mimed the movement for everyone's benefit.

"I ... ." Maddie pulled up short when she caught sight of Nick and Cassidy. "Nicky."

"Mad," Nick said. "Maude."

"Tell her that a young man is flattered when a woman comments on his butt," Maude ordered.

"I've always liked it," Nick said.

Maude patted Nick's rear end for emphasis. "See. Nick knows how important self-esteem is. That's nice, by the way."

Nick's cheeks colored. "I ... thank you."

"You've embarrassed him," Maddie said. "Look at his poor face."

Maude clapped his cheek. "He has a handsome face. He always did. Even as a child he was beautiful."

Maddie rolled her eyes. "Oh, whatever." She shifted uncomfortably when she met Cassidy's hostile gaze. "So, um, are you guys on a date?"

"I told you this afternoon we had a romantic date," Cassidy said.

"You're at Ruby Tuesday's," Maude snorted. "That's not romantic. It's filling and delicious, but it's not romantic."

"Granny," Maddie scolded. "I'm sorry. She ... ."

"It's fine," Nick said, waving off Maddie's apology. "Maude is always going to be Maude. That's why I love her."

"You're a sweet talker," Maude said. "So, should we all get a table together?"

Maddie was immediately shaking her head. "That's probably a bad idea."

"No, it's a great idea," Cassidy said, straightening her shoulders. "I would love to hear about Nick's great rescue, and I still haven't heard all of the stories from your childhood. I want to know everything about Nick."

Nick swallowed hard. "Cassidy ... I ... that wasn't what I had in mind." He shot a small look in Maddie's direction. "I think we have some things to discuss."

"And we can discuss them later," Cassidy said. "Let's all have dinner. Together. Let's all have dinner together. It sounds like fun."

Nick knew what she was doing. She was delaying the inevitable. He had no idea what she hoped to accomplish with the maneuver, but he did know if he put up a fight it would result in a scene. "Yeah. Let's all have dinner together. This is exactly how I saw this night going."

SO, what was it like to die?" Cassidy shot the first arrow, and it was aimed directly at Maddie's heart. "Did you see your mother?"

"What the ... ?" Nick was frustrated.

"Oh, I'm sorry," Cassidy said, her voice full of faux contrition. "Is that hard for you to think about?"

Since Maddie had seen her mother, the question was more annoying than anything else. "I don't think I really died," Maddie said. "I lost consciousness."

"I heard Nick had to perform CPR."

"I did," Nick said, irritated. "She wasn't breathing when I pulled her out of the water. She wasn't dead, though. The water was frigid. It slowed her body functions down."

"Oh, well, that sounds exciting," Cassidy said, nonplussed. "Did you see anything when you lost consciousness?"

Maddie shook her head. "I ... ."

"She doesn't want to talk about it," Nick snapped. "Leave her alone."

"I thought we were just having polite dinner conversation," Cassidy said, feigning innocence. "I'm sorry. Let's talk about something else. What did you and Nick do as kids?"

Maddie's face was a mask of concern, so Nick answered.

"We played in the woods."

"What did you play?"

"Lots of things," Nick said.

"Cops and robbers," Maddie supplied, a hint of a smile on her face.

"Cops and robbers," Nick agreed, finding solace in the smile. "We also played war and would lob pine cones at each other."

"I remember when you guys used to watch that crocodile man show," Maude said. "The one who always said 'crikey.'"

"Steve Irwin," Nick said, laughing. "Yeah, we got kind of rambunctious after watching that show. It was impossible not to."

"We went down to the lake and you wrestled turtles for me," Maddie teased.

"They were fearsome beasts," Nick said, holding up his hand and displaying a small scar as proof. "They're vicious biters."

"Oh, you two and the turtles," Maude said. "Maddie tried to keep the first ten you caught for her, but they were too much work. Finally, Olivia convinced Maddie that catch-and-release was the best method for enjoyment."

"Then I started finding cats for her," Nick said, smirking.

"Yes. We had three of them before Olivia put her foot down," Maude said.

"Maddie loved animals," Nick said.

"I still do," Maddie said. "I've been thinking of getting a dog."

"No dogs," Maude said. "They slobber all over you."

"Then I'm going to get a cat," Maddie warned. "The house is too lonely with just the two of us."

"Can't you get a goldfish?"

"No."

"Why not?" Maude challenged.

"You can't cuddle up with a goldfish."

"They also don't shed," Maude pointed out.

While Nick was charmed with the interplay, Cassidy was anything but. "So, did you guys have sleepovers?"

Nick shifted in his chair. "What does that matter?"

"Well, you guys are of the opposite sex. Did your mother allow Maddie to spend the night at your house?"

"She did," Nick said. "I spent the night at Maddie's all the time, too."

"How long did that last?"

Nick met Cassidy's challenging gaze. "Until Maddie left for college."

Cassidy snorted. "Her mother let you sleep in the same room with her when you were teenagers?"

"We slept in the window seat," Nick corrected. "I don't see why that's an issue."

"It's just ... I mean ... no offense to your daughter, Mrs. Graves, but didn't it bother her that these two were so ... connected?"

"No," Maude said, reading between the lines of Cassidy's inference. "They were good kids. They read a book, and then they went to sleep."

"That's what they told you," Cassidy said. "How do you know they weren't doing other things?"

She was bitter. He'd made her bitter. Nick was ashamed. In his efforts to avoid being the bad guy, he'd been the worst guy. Cassidy was so insecure, she'd turned mean and nasty. Unfortunately, her vitriol was directed in Maddie's direction.

"We just knew," Maude said, her eyes serious. "You have to trust people. Nick and Maddie never once gave us a reason to doubt them."

"And you're being incredibly nasty," Nick said, focusing on Cassidy. "What is your deal?" He knew what her deal was, but he was hoping being called on her bad behavior would force her to rein it in – at least for a few hours.

Cassidy's face contorted. "I ... I'm sorry. I have no idea why I said that."

Maude opened her mouth to say something, but Maddie shook her head quickly. Now wasn't the time.

"So, what are you guys doing over here tonight?" Nick asked, grasping for a topic of conversation that wouldn't set Cassidy off.

"We had to buy some air-conditioning units," Maddie said. "The house is unbearable."

"How many did you get?"

"Four. One for my bedroom, one for Granny's, one for the kitchen, and one for the store," Maddie replied.

"That's probably a good idea," Nick said, watching Cassidy out of the corner of his eye.

"They're heavy, though," Maude said. "We had to bribe the kid at the store to put them in our car."

"I'll manage," Maddie said. "I'll do them one at a time."

"You're still recovering," Maude challenged. "The doctor said you have to take it easy."

"Granny, I'm fine."

"No, she's right," Nick said. "After dinner, I'll stop by the house and help you. It won't take me very long."

"You don't have to do that, Nicky," Maddie said. "I know you have a ... date."

Nick faltered, the meaning behind Maddie's words washing over him. "Right. I ... ."

"We'll both come and help," Cassidy said. "With three of us working, it will take even less time."

Nick scowled. "I can drop you off at home first."

"No," Cassidy said, resolute. "This way, we can get the air-conditioning units in place and still have some time to spend together. Isn't that what you want?"

Nick was caught. "Um ... yeah."

This night just kept getting worse and worse.

6. SIX

"Your house is beautiful," Cassidy said, looking around the kitchen curiously. "I've never seen it, beyond the store, that is."

"Oh, did you visit the store when my mother was alive?" The surreal situation Maddie found herself in was making her uncomfortable. Cassidy was being far too nice, and she was far too keen on conversation. Nick's rigid shoulders told Maddie that he was struggling with the situation himself.

"I came in a few times," Cassidy said. "I wanted to meet your mother. Everyone I met in town kept telling me how close you and Nick were. I just wanted to see the store. I heard Nick spent a lot of time here when he was a kid."

"He did," Maude said, glancing between Nick and Maddie worriedly. "He'd eat entire pies by himself."

"That's because Olivia was the best baker ever," Nick said. "She always knew exactly what pie to make me when I was in a bad mood."

Maddie snorted. "You would have eaten any pie she made."

"This is true," Nick said, bending down to hoist an air-conditioning unit out of a box. "Blackberry was my favorite. She would send us out to pick blackberries, and when we brought them back, she would make a big pie for us.

"Then, a few weeks later, she would always surprise me with homemade blackberry jam," he said. "I loved summers with your mom."

"She was great," Maddie said, her gaze distant. Her mother's ghost was still hanging around, but it wasn't the same as having a flesh-and-blood person who could hold her.

"Oh, I'm sorry, Mad," Nick said. "I shouldn't have brought her up."

"No," Maddie said, shaking her head. "I like to hear stories about her. It just made me think of her for a second. Maybe we could make some jam this summer? I've never done it, but she left me a whole book of recipes."

Nick snickered. "You can't cook."

"I can cook," Maddie protested.

"What have you ever cooked?"

"I cooked you pancakes a couple of weeks ago," Maddie pointed out. "I even put blueberries in them. I didn't hear you complaining."

"I stand corrected," Nick said. "Lift that screen up, will you?"

Cassidy's gaze shifted between the two friends. "When did you make him breakfast?"

Maddie faltered. "Oh, um ... ."

"What does it matter?" Nick snapped. The hurt look on Cassidy's face told him his words were harsh, but he was so annoyed with her insistence on inviting herself into Maddie's home he could barely think straight.

"I was just asking a question," Cassidy said.

"Well, don't," Nick replied, grunting as he settled the unit in the window. "Hold this here, Mad."

Maddie did as instructed, watching as Nick fastened the unit in the window.

"Okay," he said. "Let it go and pull the window down snug on top." Nick studied his handiwork for a moment. "I am awesome."

"Yes, you should have one of those home improvement shows," Maddie teased.

"Maude, I'm trusting you to stuff that foam stuff in around the edges," Nick said.

Maude saluted. "Yes, sir."

"Let's move upstairs," Nick said.

"I can help carry the units up," Cassidy volunteered.

"There's only two of them," Nick said. "Why don't you stay down here and make sure that it's working properly?"

Cassidy's face was conflicted. "I ... ."

"I've got some nice iced tea," Maude said. "The rooms up there are small. We'll just be getting in their way."

Cassidy pressed her lips together, caught. "Of course."

MAUDE FILLED two glasses with ice cubes and tea and then settled in one of the open chairs at the dining room table. She pushed one of the glasses toward Cassidy, who was nervously fidgeting in another chair.

"Do you want to talk about it?" Maude asked.

Cassidy jerked her head up. "Talk about what?"

"Cassidy, I don't know you very well," Maude said. "What I do know doesn't seem to mesh with the woman I've seen tonight. I think you've got a lot on your mind. I have a feeling I know exactly what it is that's bothering you, too. You might as well get it off your chest."

"I don't know what you're talking about."

"Oh, girl, I'm too old to play games," Maude said. "I can see you've got your claws out and you're digging into Nick's flesh like you think someone is about to snatch him away. The problem is, he's already gone."

"What are you talking about? He took me out for a romantic dinner tonight. He's not gone. He's mine."

Maude sighed. "I know you're desperate to hold onto Nick, but you can't. Deep down, you know that, right?"

"You're just saying that because you want your precious granddaughter to win," Cassidy spat.

"Love isn't a prize," Maude said. "Love just ... is. You have to know that Nick doesn't love you. He never did. I'm not saying that to hurt you. It's important that you get some perspective, though. You're only hurting yourself by acting this way."

"And what way am I acting?" Cassidy asked.

"Like a woman who has already lost and can't admit it," Maude said. "Just ... think about it. Do you really want to try and force Nick to stay when he obviously wants to go?"

"That is not what I'm doing." Cassidy's eyes were swimming with tears. "That is not what I'm doing."

"BALANCE it on your thigh right there," Nick said, grunting as he hefted the rectangular unit into Maddie's bedroom window. "They just keep getting heavier."

"I thought you worked out," Maddie said. Her tone was teasing, but she was working so hard she was dripping with sweat. Her bedroom had always been tiny, and Maude had been urging her to move to her mother's larger room, but Maddie was reluctant to change anything about the house she loved so much.

"I do work out," Nick said, slipping the unit into the window. "Okay, hold it here while I secure it."

"Okay."

Nick leaned around her with the screwdriver and bolt, sucking in a breath when his mouth moved to within kissing distance of Maddie's plump, pink lips. For a moment, he was lost in the emotion associated with their close proximity. If he moved his lips, just a little, he would finally be able to get the one thing he'd always wanted.

"Nick." Maddie's voice was strained, her eyes wide as his face hovered right in front of her.

"Yeah."

"I ... um ... my hands are really sweaty."

"I think we're both really sweaty," Nick said, his eyes boring into her lips as she nervously ran her tongue between them. "It's ... is it getting hotter in here?"

"I really think I'm going to drop this," Maddie said.

"Oh," Nick said, snapping back to reality. "One minute, Mad. One minute."

"I THINK you're just saying this to me because you want me to walk away from Nick," Cassidy said, her heart clenching with a mixture of terror and rage. "If I walk away, then Maddie will have a clear shot at Nick."

"Maddie already has a clear shot at Nick," Maude said. "That's what you don't seem to understand."

"They're friends," Cassidy said. "They've always just been friends. They never dated." Cassidy knew she was grasping at straws.

"That doesn't mean they don't love each other," Maude said. "Cassidy, I know you're very upset, and you feel as if you're losing something here. You're not losing anything, though. He was never yours."

"We've been dating for seven months." Cassidy's voice sounded shrill, even to her own ears.

"He was still never yours," Maude said. "He and Maddie are like magnets. They were both too scared to admit how they felt about each other when they were in high school. They're adults now. There's nothing that will keep them apart. It's not a question of if. It's a question of when."

"He's with me," Cassidy argued.

"For how long?"

"You don't know," Cassidy said. "We could get married."

Maude shook her head. "Something tells me you don't believe that," she said. "You know as well as I do that he was going to break up with you tonight. That's why you insisted on coming here with us. You knew he wouldn't do it with an audience. You're trying to buy time. For what, I don't know. You really are just hurting yourself."

Cassidy's heart was beating so hard she thought she was going to pass out. She jumped to her feet, tipping over the glass of iced tea in her haste. "You have no idea what you're talking about. You're just a liar. I know what you're trying to do, and it's not going to work on me. You have no idea who you're dealing with."

· · ·

"IT'S SECURE," Nick said, tugging on the air-conditioning unit briefly. "Pull the window down."

"I can't believe how much work that was," Maddie said, grabbing the foam strips and shoving them into the creases between the frame and the metal walls of the unit. "I wouldn't have been able to do it without you."

"I think you can do anything you set your mind to, Mad," Nick said, smiling when she straightened. "Your face is red. It looks like you just ran a marathon."

"That's what it feels like."

Nick's hands rose and cupped the back of Maddie's head before he even realized what he was doing. He tilted her chin up, the sea blue of her eyes bombarding him with unasked questions. He moved in closer, but instead of kissing her, he rested his moist forehead against hers.

"W-w-what are you doing?" Maddie asked, uncertain.

"I have no idea," Nick admitted.

"I ... ." Maddie broke off.

"What were you going to say?" Nick asked, refusing to break from the position they were standing in.

"I'm not sure."

Nick snorted. "We're quite the pair."

"Nick, you know we can't ... not while ... not now."

"I know," Nick said. "I've got to get this Cassidy situation under control."

"I'm sorry things worked out this way," Maddie said. "If we hadn't ended up at the same restaurant, this would probably already be over. I didn't expect Cassidy to volunteer to come with us."

"She's desperate," Nick said. "She knows what's coming, and yet she just won't accept it. It's ... pathetic."

"Nicky," Maddie chided. "She's just sad."

"I know," Nick said. "I know I'm the one in the wrong here. She's just making things so hard."

"You just have to deal with it," Maddie said. "You don't have to deal with it tonight. It's not like you're on a timetable."

Nick pressed his eyes shut briefly. He wasn't on a timetable, but he was running out of time all the same. He wouldn't be able to stop himself from kissing Maddie again, and he wanted their first kiss to be something special. It wouldn't be if he was still joined with Cassidy, even if it was in name only. "I do have to deal with it tonight," Nick said, finally pulling his forehead back so he could brush his lips against the wrinkled spot between her eyebrows "I'm not putting this off any longer."

"Okay," Maddie said. "Um ... thank you for all your help."

Nick grinned. "At least you'll get a good night's sleep tonight," he said. "The only thing sweaty will be your dreams."

Maddie lowered her eyes, flustered. Nick knew his comment was pointed, but he liked to watch her fidget.

"You're being awfully forward when your girlfriend is down in my kitchen," Maddie challenged.

Nick's smile faltered. "Yeah. I need to go and deal with that right now." He moved out of Maddie's bedroom, casting one last longing look in the direction of her bed and then stepped into the hallway. "Tomorrow, you and I are going to have a talk, too."

Maddie stilled. "About what?"

"Something fun," Nick said. "I promise."

Maddie followed him downstairs and into the kitchen, pulling up short when she caught sight of Maude cleaning up spilled iced tea. "What happened?"

"Where's Cassidy?" Nick asked.

"She ran out," Maude said.

"Why?" Maddie pressed.

"We were just talking about a few things," Maude hedged.

"Like what?"

"About the future of her relationship with Nick," Maude admitted.

Maddie was mortified. "Granny! That's none of your business."

"Where did she go?" Nick asked.

"She ran out," Maude said. "I think ... I think she knew you were going to have a serious talk on the way home, and she didn't want to deal with it."

Nick raised his eyebrows. "You mean she *left* left?"

"I think so," Maude.

"Well ... crap," Nick said, rubbing the back of his neck. "What is she going to do? Does she think hiding is going to change something?"

"You'll have to ask her," Maude said.

"This is just unbelievable," Nick grumbled. "I can't catch a break."

"Or a breakup," Maddie said, her tone dry.

Despite himself, Nick barked out a hoarse laugh. "Good grief. It never ends."

7. SEVEN

Nick took a chance when he left Maddie's house, following the route Cassidy would have walked if she wanted to return home. He didn't see her, and when he pulled into her driveway, the small ranch was dark.

Nick considered his options: He could wait here until she returned, or he could leave and gather his strength to fight another day. He opted to wait. He was sick of playing games.

Cassidy didn't have a lot of options. She had friends in town, but she was still an outsider. Blackstone Bay was an insulated community. People were friendly to newcomers, but you didn't really belong unless you were born here.

Where would she go? For all Nick knew, she was already home and hiding in the dark. That was a disheartening thought. Would she really go that far? Nick wanted to end things, and he wanted to end them now.

He was emotionally overwrought, and it wasn't just because Cassidy was about to get her heart broken. He was tired of putting his own happiness on the backburner. When Maddie had first returned to town, he'd realized immediately he was still in love with her. The mere sight of her heart-shaped face nearly undid him. They had things to work out, though, and when Maddie finally admitted the big secret to him, he'd been relieved. He could deal with psychic visions and ghosts. He could not deal with losing her. Not again.

At first he'd held off on breaking up with Cassidy because he knew the town harpies would blame Maddie. He was hoping, with a little time, the onus of his decision would shift from her slight shoulders and land where it belonged – on him. The longer he waited, though, the harder things got.

He'd already been disassociating himself from Cassidy when Maddie returned to town. Cassidy may have convinced herself otherwise, but it was the truth. He'd been laying the groundwork for the big goodbye when Maddie's timid hello had practically knocked him on his ass. At first, he kept Cassidy in play because he didn't want an open door to Maddie. Now, all he wanted was to close the door and lock himself in a room with Maddie.

He was ready to claim the woman he loved. He just had to crush another woman to do it. It wasn't lost on Nick that he was treating Cassidy abysmally. He felt shame for it. He also felt anger that she purposely kept trying to wedge herself between him and the one thing in this world he'd always loved without reserve or question. That anger was quickly turning into resentment. Part of Nick blamed Cassidy because he wasn't back in Maddie's room with her right now.

In his head, he knew Cassidy wasn't to blame for any of this. In his heart, he knew he needed Maddie. That's all he needed. Everything else would come in time. He needed to tell Maddie how he felt and listen when she told him how she felt. He could be getting ahead of himself, he internally cautioned his excited heart. There was every possibility that Maddie didn't feel the same way about him.

He didn't believe that, though. Some things are destiny, and Maddie Graves was Nick's destiny. He had always believed that, and he still did.

After two hours had passed, Nick fired up the engine of his truck and pulled out of Cassidy's driveway. As long as he was sitting there, Cassidy wasn't going to come home. He didn't know how he knew that. He just did.

Tomorrow was a new day. He would figure out what to do then.

Had Nick been paying closer attention when his headlights flashed on the front of Cassidy's house, he would have noticed a shaking figure as it stood in front of the glass and peered outside. He didn't, though, and Cassidy had earned another reprieve.

For now.

MADDIE'S DREAMS were sweaty that night, just not in the way Nick had insinuated earlier in the evening. After an hour of letting the air conditioner work its magic, and a stern lecture to Maude about butting into other people's business, Maddie passed out in a puddle of sheer exhaustion.

Being around Nick was draining. Wanting to touch him, and constantly fighting those urges, made her mind as tired as her body. She was ready for Nick to be free, even if it meant they wouldn't be together.

Nick had been acting differently toward her for weeks. He'd always been attentive, but now it was as if they were in sync. He would reach for her, but she'd already be reaching for him so they'd meet halfway. Once there were no secrets between them, it was as if Nick wanted to eliminate all of the space between them, too.

His presence was enough to steal the oxygen from her lungs.

Even if they couldn't be together, Maddie wanted the option of exploration. She needed to know if they truly were meant for each other because she could never move on otherwise.

Maddie expected to slip into a naughty dream about Nick, cool lake water and feverish skin colliding in her subconscious mind. Instead, she got something else. Something terrifying. At first Maddie thought she was the center of the dream. She knew she was in danger, the darkened Blackstone Bay streets closing in on her as she scampered toward safety.

Maddie allowed herself to relax into the vision. She had no idea where safety was, or why she was heading in this direction. Since Maddie had found herself a visitor in the nightmares of others before

– an unwilling participant in scenes from their future – it didn't take her long to adjust to what she was seeing.

This wasn't her dream. This wasn't even Tara Warner's dream. No, this was Tara Warner's future, and she needed to pay attention.

The night was hot and sweaty, the heat so oppressive Maddie could feel the perspiration trickling down the back of her neck. It was late, and a quick glance at the moon told her the sun had set hours before. Why would Tara be out this late alone?

The echoing sound of footsteps on the pavement behind her caused Maddie to swivel, her eyes searching the street behind her but coming up empty. Someone was there. She couldn't see who, but she could ... feel ... someone.

"Who's there?"

Nothing.

"I know you're there. Come out so I can see you." Maddie had never been able to control a vision. That didn't stop her from trying every time she got the chance. "I just want to see you. You don't have to talk if you don't want to."

Silence.

"I ... ." Maddie broke off. She could hear breathing, and it was much closer than it should be. A hand reached out in the darkness. Maddie could see it in her mind, even though her dream-vision eyes were blind. Maddie jerked away, stumbling and then ... .

Maddie bolted upright in her bed, her breath coming out in rapid gasps as her heart hammered.

The morning light was filtering through her shaded windows, and as the dream subsided into memory, Maddie fought to anchor herself to reality. What did she know? The moon. It had been full. When was the next full moon?

She grabbed her cell phone off of her nightstand and pulled up the calendar, paging forward to see that the full moon was still a few days away. Of course, just because the moon looked full in the dream, that didn't mean it was an actual full moon. The time frame could easily encompass the days leading up to the full moon, and the days after. She just didn't know.

Maddie tossed the covers off of her and climbed out of bed. When she opened the door to the hallway, a wall of heat hit her. Air conditioning had already spoiled her. She'd forgotten how hot the rest of the house was. "Ugh."

Instead of heading straight downstairs for breakfast, where she was sure a cantankerous Maude was waiting, Maddie detoured into the bathroom. She needed a lukewarm shower and twenty minutes to think. There had to be hints in the vision. She just needed time to absorb them.

"THE WORLD IS COMING TO AN END!"

Maddie raised an eyebrow in her grandmother's direction as she walked into the kitchen about a forty-five minutes later. "Zombie apocalypse?"

"What?" Maude wasn't alone. Her longtime friend, Irma Kingston, was sitting at the table, and the two women had their heads bent together as they studied a sheet of paper.

"You said the world was coming to an end," Maddie said dryly, considering the coffee pot for a moment before moving over to the refrigerator and snagging a bottle of water. "I was just wondering if the zombie apocalypse was finally here."

"Your sense of humor rears up at the oddest of times," Maude said, wrinkling her nose.

"So I've been told," Maddie said. "Irma, it's nice to see you."

Irma didn't bother looking up from the sheet of paper. "I'm glad you came home. It's about time."

Sometimes Maddie thought Irma and Maude shared a personality. When they were in the same room, that personality was amplified times ten. "I agree," Maddie said, pasting a smile on her face. "Do you two want breakfast?"

"We don't have time to eat," Maude said. "Didn't you hear me? The world is coming to an end."

Maddie rolled her eyes. "Okay. I'm all ears. What's wrong now?"

"Brace yourself."

Maddie made a face. "I'm braced."

"Harriet Proctor wants to be a Pink Lady."

Maddie was confused. She knew who Harriet Proctor was. In addition to being Maude's lifelong nemesis – there was even a rumor about Harriet trying to seduce Maddie's late grandfather – Harriet was also Marla Proctor's grandmother. "Is that a euphemism for something?"

"Of course not," Maude said, irked. "She wants to be a Pink Lady."

"I don't understand what that means," Maddie admitted.

"It means that she's applied for membership to our group."

Maddie searched her memory. "Oh, you mean the Red Hat Society? I thought that was the name of your group."

"We changed it five years ago," Maude snapped. "Keep up."

"I'm sorry." Maddie held her hands up in mock surrender. "What's it called now?"

"The Pink Lady Society."

"Ah. Fun. Why did you change the name?"

"Because we found out that there was another Red Hat Society," Maude said. "Did you know that?"

Maddie smirked. "I might have heard something about it."

"Well, we didn't know," Maude said. "Do you know what those women do?"

"I think they wear red hats and purple dresses ... and drink tea. Is that right?"

"Yeah. Tea." Maude's voice was positively dripping with disdain.

Maddie waited.

"Tea!"

"What's wrong with that? You like tea."

"I do," Maude said. "I also like bourbon in it. It seems the proper Red Hat Society ladies frown on putting bourbon in your tea. They threatened to go after us if we didn't change our name. Have you ever heard anything so ridiculous?"

Maddie swallowed the mad urge to laugh. "I guess not. So, now you're a Pink Lady? That sounds fun."

"It was until Harriet Proctor petitioned our board for membership."

"You have a board?"

"Of course we have a board," Maude said. "We're a very important group."

"So, just vote against her," Maddie suggested.

"Oh, I hadn't thought of that," Maude said, angry.

"There's no reason to be sarcastic," Maddie chided.

"I'm sorry," Maude replied primly. "You just don't understand the ramifications if Harriet becomes a Pink Lady."

"Zombie apocalypse?" Maddie was starting to enjoy herself.

"Don't you have somewhere to be?" Maude asked wearily.

As a matter of fact, she did. "Okay. I'm going. Be good you two. If you get arrested, I won't be able to bail you out until this afternoon."

"That's fine," Maude said. "It's Thursday. They have turkey in the jail on Thursdays."

Maddie didn't want to know how her grandmother knew that. "Just ... be good."

8. EIGHT

Tara Warner's pretty features were welcoming when the bell over the flower shop door jangled. When she saw Maddie standing there, though, her smile started to slip.

"Ms. Graves, what a surprise."

"Call me Maddie."

"Maddie." Tara's face was conflicted. "I ... do you need some flowers?"

Maddie internally chastised herself for not coming up with a suitable lie before entering the store. "Yes. I'm looking for something for my grandmother. I think she's about to have a bad day." That wasn't a total lie. If Maude was to be believed, the world was coming to an end. That constituted a bad day in anyone's book.

"Maude? What's wrong now?" Tara visibly relaxed at Maddie's admission.

"I don't know. Irma Kingston is over at the house and they claim the world is going to end because Harriet Proctor wants to be a Pink Lady."

Tara snickered. "That sounds just about right. What kind of flowers does Maude like?"

"I don't really know," Maddie said. "I just wanted to get her something to make her feel better, and it's not like there are a lot of shopping options in town. It was either this or a milkshake, and the milkshake would melt before I could get it home."

"Well, the flowers aren't doing much better in the heat," Tara admitted. "How about a nice potted hydrangea? You can put it in the yard and they grow beautifully in the soil up here."

"That sounds great," Maddie said. "What colors do you have?"

"We have pretty much everything," Tara said. "Keep in mind, the color doesn't always stay the same. It depends on the soil it's planted in."

"Oh, I didn't know that," Maddie said. "That's interesting. Well, give me a blue one for now. It will match Granny's mood. If it changes color, I'll tell her it's like a mood ring."

Tara giggled. "I just love your grandmother. She's such a bundle of energy."

"She is," Maddie agreed. "Sometimes I wish she'd take a nap, though."

"She was really sad after Olivia died," Tara said carefully.

"I know. I should have come home sooner. It took me a few weeks to get everything in order so I could come back. It took longer than I would have liked."

"Nick Winters spent a lot of time with her." Tara was watching Maddie, waiting for a reaction.

"That sounds like him," Maddie said, her face placid.

"People say you two were really close when you were growing up," Tara said.

"We were."

"People also say it's only a matter of time until you're really close in another way."

Maddie pressed her lips together, considering. "People say a lot, don't they?"

"Just for the record, you should know that Cassidy is one of my closest friends," Tara said.

"Cassidy is a nice woman."

"She is," Tara agreed. "She's been a little worked up about Nick lately."

"That's really none of my business," Maddie said. "Nick's relationships are his to deal with."

"Cassidy is convinced that you're trying to steal Nick from her," Tara said. "Is that the truth?"

Maddie furrowed her brow. "I don't want to get into this conversation. Rest assured, the last thing I want is for anyone to get hurt – especially Cassidy."

"I thought she was overreacting," Tara said. "The problem is, Nick is known for having a certain reputation in this town. Cassidy knew it when she started dating him. She knew he had a particular ... schedule ... he adhered to. She thought she would be the one to outlive the schedule."

"Like I said, this is Nick's ... ."

Tara held up her hand to still Maddie. "Cassidy and I bonded because we were both outsiders," Tara said. "I had ties to the town. Cassidy didn't. I knew how insular everyone was here, but I always loved the town. Even when I visited as a teenager, you and Nick were something of an enigma."

"People didn't understand why we were so close," Maddie said. "Nick was cool, and I wasn't. That confused people."

"I think people understood why you and Nick were so close," Tara said, wrinkling her nose. "What they didn't understand is why neither one of you acted on it."

Maddie shifted uncomfortably. "I'm not sure why you're telling me this now," she said. "You were in my shop two days ago and you never brought any of this up."

"That's because Cassidy didn't call me sobbing two days ago," Tara said.

"Did she go to your house last night? She left and we couldn't find her."

"She didn't come to my house," Tara said. "We just talked on the phone for a few hours. She says that Nick is confused and that he's going to make the biggest mistake of his life and throw her away so he can have you."

Maddie didn't reply.

"The thing is, I think Nick was going to throw Cassidy away before you even returned," Tara said, her expression serious. "Your return confused him, and even messed him up a little bit, so he let things ride. Now he's ready to get back on track, and Cassidy can't see the reality of the situation."

"And what reality is that?" Maddie asked.

"Nick was just waiting for you to come back," Tara said. "He never let himself get close to anyone because they weren't you. I'm not involved in the situation like Cassidy is, so I can see it for what it is."

"I don't want Cassidy to get hurt," Maddie said. "I really don't."

"I believe you," Tara said. "I just need you to know that, when this all goes down, I don't hate you. I do have to be Cassidy's friend, though. I have to take her side."

"I understand that."

"Good," Tara said, exhaling heavily. "I'm glad we got this chance to talk. For a second, when I saw you at the door, I thought you were here to give me some bad news about my reading the other day."

Maddie forced herself to remain calm. "What do you mean?"

"You just seemed to lose yourself a little during the reading," Tara said, shrugging as she punched a few numbers into the cash register. "I know it's silly, but I thought you might have seen something bad and then decided not to tell me."

Maddie's smile was watery. "I wouldn't be a very good psychic if I kept something like that from you, would I?"

"Oh, I don't know," Tara said, pushing the potted hydrangea across the counter. "I would think a good psychic is also someone who doesn't want to hurt anyone. Oh, well, it doesn't matter now. Tell Maude I hope she beats Harriet into the dirt."

Maddie grinned. "Oh, trust me, that's exactly what she has planned."

"WHAT IS THAT?" Maude eyed the hydrangea like it had eight legs and pinchers.

"It's a plant to make you feel better," Maddie replied, scanning the kitchen. "Is Irma still here?"

"She had to do some reconnaissance. What am I supposed to do with this plant? And why do you think I feel bad?"

"Actually, I just needed a reason to go into the flower shop," Maddie admitted. "I wanted to talk to Tara Warner. Buying a plant for you was my excuse. What kind of reconnaissance?"

Maude ignored the question. "Oh, good. I was hoping you hadn't lost your mind and thought a plant would really cheer me up. Can I kill it?"

"No. I'm going to plant it in the yard," Maddie said. "Don't you dare kill it."

"So, did you get any information out of Tara?"

"No," Maddie said. "I had a dream about her last night, though."

"A dream, or a vision?"

"Vision."

"And?"

"And at some point in the next few days, when the moon is full, she's going to be walking downtown and someone is going to be following her," Maddie said.

"Following her, or killing her?"

"I woke up when he grabbed her in the dream," Maddie said. "I can't be sure what happens after."

"When you get these visions, do they always come true?"

"Unless I do something to stop them."

"How many of them have you been able to stop?"

"A few," Maddie said. "Not nearly enough."

Maude patted Maddie's arm. "You can only do what you can do, Maddie. Have you mentioned this to Nick?"

"I told him at the lake the other night," Maddie replied. "He said he was going to try to talk to Tara, but that was before the whole Cassidy snafu. Did you know Cassidy and Tara were friends, by the way?"

Maude knit her eyebrows together. "Now that you mention it, I guess I did. You know how outsiders congregate together. Why? What happened?"

"It wasn't anything bad," Maddie said. "She just wanted me to know that she's going to take Cassidy's side when Nick breaks up with her."

"Did Cassidy tell her Nick was going to break up with her?"

Maddie shrugged. "Tara said Cassidy called her in tears last night. It didn't sound like Nick found her so he could break up with her, more that Cassidy suspected he was going to break up with her."

"I can't believe Nick hasn't dumped her yet," Maude grumbled. "It would be just like him to drag this out forever because he doesn't want to be the bad guy."

Maddie's heart jolted. "Are you saying you think Nick isn't going to break up with her?"

"No," Maude said. "I'm saying I think Nick is the bravest emotional coward I've ever met. He's going to break up with her. Of course, she's going to keep hiding. It could take weeks at this rate."

Maddie frowned. "You're a ray of sunshine, Granny."

"I'm sorry," Maude said.

"It's fine." The bell over the front door of the store jangled, and Maddie moved from the kitchen to the front of the house. She was surprised to find Catherine Brooks, one of Maude's cohorts, waiting for them. "Ms. Brooks."

Maude pushed past Maddie and stormed into the store. "Did you hear?"

"I heard," Catherine said.

"What are we going to do about it?"

"We're going to figure it out." Maddie had always liked Catherine. The woman was as calm as Maude was feisty. At least there was one member of Maude's little group of boozehounds with a clear head on her shoulders to make sure no one did anything illegal.

"Do you two mind making your plans in the kitchen?" Maddie asked. "You're going to scare off my customers."

Maude stuck her tongue out and blew a raspberry in Maddie's direction. "Come on, Catherine."

"Actually, I'm here to talk to Maddie," Catherine said.

"You are?" Maddie was surprised.

"I am," Catherine said. "In addition to being president of the Pink Lady Society, I am also the head of the Solstice Celebration Carnival Committee."

Maddie wasn't sure what to say. "Congratulations?" Blackstone Bay was a town of festivals. They had at least seven every summer, and another two in the fall. Oh, and there was the Winter Wonderland Festival around Christmas, too. When she was younger, Maddie had enjoyed each and every one. She'd actually forgotten the Solstice Celebration was almost upon them.

"I was hoping you would set up a booth at the fair this weekend," Catherine said.

"What kind of booth?"

"A psychic booth."

Maddie balked. "What? No. That's a horrible idea."

"Why?" Catherine asked, nonplussed. "Your mother used to do it."

"She did?"

"She did."

Maddie looked to Maude for confirmation. "Really?"

Maude nodded.

"But ... a psychic booth? What would that entail?"

Catherine chuckled. "Nothing sinister. You just do tarot card readings for people. It's all fun and games. Olivia used to turn a nice profit."

"I don't know," Maddie said, stalling.

"Oh, come on, Maddie," Maude prodded. "It will do you some good. You can't hide in this house forever. Live a little."

"That's easy for you to say," Maddie shot back. "Everyone won't be looking at you."

"They won't be looking at you for anything but a good time," Catherine said, patting Maddie's shoulder. "You'll be fine. You're always such a worrywart. You should set up your booth tomorrow and have it ready by seven."

"But ... ."

Catherine started moving toward the door. "Oh, and Olivia used to dress up."

"What?" Maddie was panicked.

"Don't worry," Maude said. "I've got a Wonder Woman costume you can borrow. You'll just have to shave your legs – and your bikini region – to make sure you don't scare people away."

"I am not dressing up like Wonder Woman!"

9. NINE

Nick let himself in through the front door of Magicks, replacing the key under the ceramic turtle on the front porch before shutting and locking the door. Maddie and Maude weren't expecting him, but he was too antsy to sit home alone.

He wasn't surprised to find Maddie curled up with a book in the front window seat. Olivia had built the extended space specifically so Maddie and Nick would have a place to hang out in the store when she was working. It was Maddie's favorite spot in the house, which made it Nick's favorite spot, too.

"Hey," Maddie said, surprise washing over her face. "What are you doing here?"

"I just didn't feel like being alone," Nick said, kicking off his shoes and climbing up next to her so he could recline against the mountain of pillows.

"What's wrong?"

Nick brushed Maddie's blonde hair away from her concerned face. "Cassidy is hiding from me."

"Define hiding."

"I sat outside of her house for two hours last night," Nick said. "She didn't come home."

"Maybe she was already home."

"I thought about that," Nick said. "The idea made me ... uncomfortable. The house was dark. If she was in there, she not only knew I was sitting in the driveway, but she was also sitting in the dark so she didn't have to face me."

"I feel sorry for her," Maddie said.

"Why?"

"Because ... you know why."

"I don't until you tell me," Nick prodded.

"I went into the flower shop today," Maddie said, changing the subject.

Nick sighed. Now was not the time for a serious conversation. Delaying it was giving him an ulcer, though. "You went to see Tara?"

"Yeah. I told her I was looking for a gift for Maude because she was so upset about the Harriet situation."

"I'm almost afraid to ask," Nick said. "What's the Harriet situation?"

"Apparently she wants to be a Pink Lady. I didn't know about the Pink Lady Society until today, by the way. It seems I've been missing out."

Nick grinned. "They're very selective. I'm an honorary member."

"You are not," Maddie said, slapping his thigh playfully.

"I am. I helped Irma when she got a flat tire and she made me an honorary member," Nick said. "They all voted and everything. They tried to make me drink tea with bourbon in it."

"Did they make you dress in pink?"

"I'm far too manly to wear pink."

"Oh, I think you'd look good in pink."

Maddie's face was bare, scrubbed clean before she turned in for the evening. Her clear blue eyes were fathomless pools as she regarded him. Coming here was a bad idea, Nick realized. All he could think about was kissing her. "I look good in everything," Nick said. "And nothing."

Maddie's cheeks colored. "I'll have to take your word for it."

"No, you don't. You got to see how good I looked up close and personal the other night."

Maddie's mouth dropped open, scandalized. "I did not see you. I just ... hugged you."

"Oh, don't lie, Mad," Nick said, enjoying himself immensely. "I saw you peeking on the beach when you thought I wasn't looking."

"I did not!"

Nick tried to refrain from laughing, but he couldn't. "You're so easy."

Maddie pinched his shoulder. "You're so not funny."

"I'm a little funny," Nick said, gripping her hand tightly and pulling it up to his chest.

They rested like that for a few minutes before Maddie broke the silence. "Tara kind of gave me an earful about Cassidy."

Nick shifted slightly. "They're friends. I forgot about that. I should have warned you."

"It was okay," Maddie said. "She just kind of wanted to give me a warning."

"A warning about what?"

"She seems aware of your intentions regarding Cassidy."

"I think everyone in Blackstone Bay is aware of my intentions regarding Cassidy," Nick said. "I think Cassidy is aware, too, and that's why she's hiding. I stopped by her house twice today. I stopped by the school. She called in sick. She's literally in hiding."

"I'm sorry."

"It's not your fault, Mad. It's mine."

"If you don't want to break up with her ... ."

"Don't you dare finish that sentence," Nick said. "I want to break up with her. I want ... to move on. I'm stuck until I can see her in person."

"Well, she'll probably show up at the fair this weekend," Maddie said.

"I'm hoping I can find her before the fair tomorrow. I'd really rather not break up with her in front of hundreds of people."

"I understand."

"If I have to break up with her in front of hundreds of people, though, I'm going to do it," Nick added. "I'm just … done. I can't keep doing this. She needs to move on with her life."

"Well, you can hide here if you need to," Maddie said. "Maude isn't scared of pitchforks."

Nick snickered, lifting his head when Maude noisily clomped into the room. "Speak of the devil."

"You were talking about Harriet Proctor?" Maude deadpanned.

"We were," Nick said, playing along.

"Well, I have an idea about that," Maude said, focusing on Maddie. "When she comes to your booth, and she will come because she knows it bugs me, I want you to tell her she's going to die of the herpes."

Maddie rolled her eyes. "I'm not going to tell her that. You don't die from herpes."

"How do you know?" Maude asked, narrowing her eyes.

"Yeah, Mad, how do you know that?" Nick teased.

Maddie poked him in the ribs. "You're on thin ice, buddy."

"Then tell her she's going to die of Chlamydia," Maude said. "I'm not particular."

"First of all, I haven't even decided if I'm going to run a booth," Maddie argued.

"You told Catherine you would."

"I did not," Maddie said. "You two ambushed me and told me what I would be doing. I never agreed to it."

"Well, you're doing it," Maude said. "I'll look bad if you back out now."

"I'm not sure I'm comfortable with it," Maddie said.

"What kind of booth do they want you to run?" Nick asked.

"They want me to read tarot cards for people."

"Olivia did that for a few years," Nick said. "She had a good time. She was popular."

"That's because people liked my mother."

Nick sighed and brushed his hair off his forehead. "People like you, too."

"No, they don't. They always stare at me. I can feel their eyes on me. They all think I'm ... odd."

"You are odd," Nick said. "You're also amazing and magical. Stop getting down on yourself. I thought you were going to work on your self-esteem?"

"I am. That doesn't mean I'm oblivious to people staring at me."

"They're not staring at you because you're odd anyway," Nick said.

"Oh, really? Then why are they staring at me?"

"Because you're beautiful."

Maddie froze, embarrassed pleasure climbing her cheeks. "I ... ."

"He's right," Maude said. "You just need to get over yourself. You're a beautiful girl. Men stare."

"Women stare, too."

"Because they're jealous," Nick said.

"You're making that up."

"No, I'm not," Nick said. "You just need to suck it up. Most of the people in this town see you for what you are: sweet and gorgeous. You're the only one who doesn't see that."

"What about Marla Proctor?"

"Tell her she has the herpes," Maude suggested.

"She probably really does," Nick said, grimacing. "Now, *she's* the devil."

"Her grandmother is the devil," Maude corrected. "Marla is just the heir apparent."

Nick snickered and then turned serious. "I think it would be good for you to do the booth," he said. "You need to put yourself out there a little more. It's not good to surround yourself with three people and try to live in a small corner of town."

"I surround myself with more than three people," Maddie protested.

"You've got Maude, Christy and me," Nick countered. "Who else?"

"Mom."

"Okay, four," Nick conceded. "Unfortunately, the fourth is someone only you can see."

"That doesn't mean she's not important to me."

"Of course she is," Nick said, tugging on Maddie's hair so she would focus on him. "I'm not saying she's not important. I'm just saying it would do you some good to get out and have some fun."

"How do you know it will be fun?"

"Because, when you're done, I'm going to take you to the fair and buy you an elephant ear," Nick said. "I might even win you a stuffed animal if you're a very good girl."

Maddie rolled her eyes. "You can't take me to the fair with the Cassidy situation still up in the air."

"Oh, good grief, you haven't handled that yet?" Maude placed her hands on her hips and fixed Nick with a pointed scowl. "Sometimes I worry that you're addled."

Nick extended his index finger. "Don't push me. I've had a horrible day."

"Cassidy has been hiding," Maddie explained. "She even called in sick to work."

"That's a bummer," Maude said. "It's downright despicable really."

"It probably wouldn't have happened if you hadn't enlightened her last night," Maddie pointed out.

"Well, live and learn," Maude said, turning back to the staircase. "I'm going to retire for the evening. I left the Wonder Woman costume on your bed, by the way. You can try it on in the morning."

"I'm not dressing up as Wonder Woman," Maddie said. "I told you that."

"Well, you have to dress up as something. That's the only costume I have."

Once Maude was gone, Nick couldn't resist chasing the costume topic. "Why does Maude have a Wonder Woman costume?"

"I'm scared to ask."

"Why does she want you to wear it?"

"Because Catherine said Mom used to dress up when she ran a booth at the festival," Maddie explained.

Nick burst into laughter, the hearty guffaws wracking his solid chest.

"It's not funny."

"Olivia dressed up like a gypsy," Nick said. "Or ... I don't know ... a fortune teller. She wore a long skirt. It had little bells on it. I remember. She jangled when she walked. I liked it. She wore some white blouse with it. It was big, and it hung off her shoulders. And then she wrapped her head in a scarf. She didn't dress up like Wonder Woman."

"Oh," Maddie said, understanding dawning. "That makes so much more sense."

Nick grinned. "It does. Although, I'm not going to lie, if you want to put on the Wonder Woman costume and show it to me, I'd be up for seeing you in it."

"You're *so* not funny," Maddie said, pouting.

"You can't wear it in front of anyone else, though," Nick said. "I couldn't take it if others saw you looking like that."

"I'm not wearing it in front of anyone. I can promise you that."

"Oh, one day you're going to wear that costume for me, Mad," Nick said. "I can guarantee it."

"Oh yeah? How can you guarantee it?"

Nick studied her face closely for a second and then slipped his arm under her and pulled her close. Their mouths were inches apart, but neither made a move to close the gap. "I just can."

He raised his chin up and gave her a soft kiss on the forehead. "Turn off the light."

"You're going to sleep here?" Maddie was surprised.

"I can't bear the thought of sleeping anywhere else," he said. "I just ... need sleep and you. Tomorrow is another day. I'm a police officer, for crying out loud. Cassidy can only hide for so long."

Maddie switched off the light and settled on her side. Nick wrapped his body around her and rested his face in the hollow of her neck. "Goodnight, my Maddie."

"Goodnight."

10. TEN

"This was a great idea," Christy said, helping Maddie level the table she'd brought from Magicks the next afternoon. "I like the tent. Where did it come from?"

Maddie lifted her head to the purple monstrosity in question and shrugged. "I have no idea. Don't you think it's a bit much?"

"It's a 'magic' tent," Christy corrected. "It's supposed to be over the top."

"There are stars on it."

"So?"

"It just makes me feel ... exposed."

"It's a tent," Christy said. "It's supposed to protect you from the elements."

"Oh! Is it supposed to rain tonight? That would great."

Christy grinned. "Clear skies all week ... and the weekend. Bummer for you."

Maddie scowled. "This is just ... too much."

"You're too much," Christy said. "You're not wearing that, are you?"

Maddie glanced down at her denim shorts and T-shirt, unsure. "I was hoping to."

"No one wants to see a psychic who dresses like a high school girl on summer break."

"It's just ... I'm not sure I'm comfortable dressing up," Maddie admitted.

"Did you bring something to dress up in?"

Maddie bit her lip and nodded.

Christy studied her for a second and then drew the flaps of the tent closed. "Get dressed. I'll watch the door until you're done."

"We haven't finished setting up yet."

"We will when you're dressed," Christy said. "The fair starts in twenty minutes. Don't make me strip you myself."

Maddie scowled, but she moved over to the bag she'd brought and opened it. She drew out the crinkly skirt – the purple one Nick had described the night before – and held it up to her slim hips.

"That was your mom's," Christy said. "I recognize it."

"Do you think she would mind if I wore it?"

"I think she would want you to wear it," Christy said. "She loved that skirt. It jangles when you walk. Did you know that?"

"Nick told me last night. That's how I knew to look for it."

"You were with Nick last night?" Christy was intrigued. "Put the skirt on. Did you bring the blouse, too?"

Maddie nodded.

"How about the scarf?"

"I ... found three of them. I wasn't sure which one was right."

Christy sighed. "I'll help you with the scarf. Put the blouse and skirt on first."

Maddie stripped out of her shorts and T-shirt and quickly pulled on the calf-length skirt and blouse. The blouse was big enough to hang off her shoulders and show off her bra.

"First off, your body is just sick," Christy said. "How often do you work out?"

"Five days a week," Maddie said. "It hasn't been as much this past week, though. It's been too hot. I did swim the other night."

"Were you alone?"

Maddie shifted. "I ... um ... ."

"That's what I thought," Christy said. "You need to wear something under that blouse. You're thinner than your mom was. Everyone will be looking down your shirt all night if you wear it that way.

"Although, if I had your body, I would want people to look down my shirt constantly," she said. "In fact, I'd stop wearing clothes altogether."

Maddie made a face. "I brought a tank top."

"Put it on," Christy instructed. "Tell me what you and Nick did last night."

"We talked and then we slept in the window seat."

"That's it?"

"That's it," Maddie said. "I hate to disappoint you, but it was a perfectly chaste evening." Intentions didn't count, she reminded herself. Yearning didn't count.

"What's the deal with Cassidy?" Christy asked, waiting until Maddie was fully clothed before drifting away from the tent flaps. "That's a great tank top. I love the sequins."

"I thought they were festive."

"They are," Christy said. "Sit down on the chair. I'll fix your hair, and then we'll finish with the tent."

Maddie obeyed.

"You were about to tell me about Cassidy," Christy prodded.

"I ... I feel really bad."

"Why?"

"Because Nick is going to break up with her," Maddie said.

"Well, Maddie, you're a beautiful girl, but Nick isn't breaking up with Cassidy just because of you," Christy said, running a brush through Maddie's long locks. "He doesn't love her."

"It feels like he's doing it for me," Maddie admitted. "It feels like ... things are changing."

Christy smiled. "Of course they're changing," she said. "There are no more obstacles between you and Nick. You told him the truth. He accepted it. All of the obstacles keeping you apart are gone. Well,

Cassidy, but she's like a speed bump. Now you two are free to be together."

"What if ... ?"

"No," Christy said, wagging her finger in Maddie's face. "No more ifs. You're dealing with *when* now, not *if*. It's okay to be happy, Maddie. It's sad Cassidy is having such a hard time, but it's not your fault."

"She's hiding from Nick," Maddie admitted. "Maude gave her an earful the other night, and Cassidy stormed out of the house because she figured out Nick was going to break up with her. She's been hiding from him ever since. She even called in sick to work."

"Oh, that's awful," Christy clucked, tying Maddie's hair up in twin buns on the side of her head and securing them loosely. "I don't even know what to say to that. It just makes her sound so ... pathetic."

"Which makes me feel like this horny ... harlot."

"Harlot? Nice word. Are you going to burn some witches at the stake soon?"

Maddie made a face. "You know what I mean."

"I do," Christy said. "I also know you're a good person, Maddie. Someone was going to get hurt in this scenario no matter what. Unfortunately, that was always going to be Cassidy. You can't fix it so you both win. Only one of you is going to win. We all knew it was going to be you."

Maddie rubbed her forehead, forcing the deep thoughts out of her mind as she focused on the evening ahead. "I can only deal with so much at one time. Let me get through tonight. I'll worry about Cassidy tomorrow."

"That sounds like a great idea."

"I WANT A TAROT CARD READING."

Maddie rolled her eyes as she regarded Marla dubiously. "You want me to give you a tarot card reading?"

"Well, me and Charles here." The man Marla was clinging to was handsome, if a little ... sterilized. That was the only word Maddie could think of when she looked at him. His hair was gelled to perfection, and even though the wind billowed occasionally though the tent, it didn't ruffle in the slightest. His face was chiseled and handsome, but there was no character to it. It was flat. His eyes were dark and expressive, and even though Marla was desperate for him to watch her, he was more interested in watching Maddie.

"Are you a psychic?" Charles asked, his tone teasing.

"I am," Maddie said, reminding herself that she was playing a part and not outing herself. "Do you want to know anything specific?"

Charles smiled, revealing a dimple in his cheek and a glint in his eyes as he took one of the open seats across from Maddie. "I want to know if I'm going to be rich forever."

Maddie bit the inside of her cheek. "Okay. How about you, Marla? What do you want to know?"

"I want to know if Charles is going to be rich forever, too."

That figured. Maddie forced her face to remain neutral. "Okay. Cut the cards."

Charles obliged. "So, did you grow up here in Blackstone Bay?"

"Yes," Maddie said, doling the cards out so she could study them. "Marla and I went to high school together."

"Oh, were you friends?"

"Definitely not."

Marla kicked her under the table. "We were friendly."

In what world? "Yeah, we were great friends."

The sarcasm wasn't lost on Charles. "I'm sensing a bit of a rivalry here."

"Oh, there was no rivalry," Marla said. "I just ran with one circle, and Maddie ran with one ... guy."

"Oh, you had a serious boyfriend?" Charles studied her naked left hand. "It seems like it didn't work out."

"The cards show a bright future for you," Maddie said, opting to make up a future instead of reading the muddled mess in front of her. It wasn't exactly bad, but it wasn't exactly good either. Since this was her last reading of the night, she just wanted to get it over with. "It seems your wealth will be growing exponentially."

Charles smirked. "Of course it will be."

"It seems you're going to have a very happy life."

"What about me?" Marla pressed.

Maddie forced herself to remain calm. "You're going to get everything you deserve, and so much more."

Marla beamed. "I knew it!"

"It seems you're a good match," Maddie added. If anyone deserved a smarmy husband with an inflated sense of ego, it was Marla. She didn't feel guilty about pushing them together.

"We're a great match," Marla said.

"Yes," Charles replied, less enthusiastic. "That's ... outstanding news."

"MY FEET ARE KILLING ME," Maddie said, stripping out of her shoes and dropping them onto the chair next to Christy as the duo surveyed the dance floor. "Now I remember why I always wear tennis shoes instead of heels."

"You did a good job, Maddie," Christy said. "I'm really proud of you."

"It wasn't a big deal."

"You didn't punch Marla," Christy pointed out. "I think you deserve an award."

Maddie glanced over her shoulder and scanned the crowd. She wouldn't admit it – even to herself – but she was looking for Nick. She was hoping he would make a grand entrance and steal her away for an elephant ear and some alone time. He was nowhere in sight, though.

"I'm sure he'll show, Maddie," Christy said, reading her expression. "Just sit back and relax. You're off the clock."

"I wasn't looking for ... anyone."

"Right."

"I wasn't."

"Listen to the music and have a drink," Christy said, gesturing to the red plastic cup she'd brought over to the table for Maddie. "If you want to get drunk, I totally encourage it.

You're within walking distance of your house. Get hammered. Let loose."

"I agree."

Maddie stilled when she heard the voice, recognizing it immediately. Charles Hawthorne III was standing about two feet away, and his gaze was fixed on Maddie. "Mr. Hawthorne," Maddie said. "It's nice to see you again."

Christy arched a quizzical eyebrow.

"This is Marla's date," Maddie said pointedly.

"Date, not husband," Charles said quickly. "This is only our second date. We barely know each other."

"Well, since you're on a date, it would probably be in your best interests to bug her," Christy said, taking an instant dislike to Charles. "We were in the middle of a conversation."

Charles shot Christy a dark look. "Actually, I was hoping the fetching psychic would grant me a dance."

Maddie froze in her chair.

"Well, how about it?"

"I ... um ... ."

"Her feet hurt," Christy said. "She's taking a rest."

"Oh, one dance won't kill her."

"No, it won't." Nick bumped Charles with his shoulder, pushing him out of the way as he approached the table. He patted Christy's shoulder in greeting and then focused on Maddie. "How was your big debut? I'm sorry I missed it."

"Who are you?" Charles asked, irritated.

"I'm Nick Winters."

"He's a police officer," Christy chimed in.

"I am," Nick said. "I'm off duty, though, and I thought I would take the opportunity to share a dance with my ... best friend."

"Best friend?" Charles looked dubious.

"Yes," Nick said, refusing to even look at him. "Come on, Mad. We haven't danced in years."

Maddie took his extended hand and let him lead her to the dance floor, secretly relieved her knight in shining armor wasn't looking tarnished in the least this evening.

Nick wrapped his arms around Maddie's waist and pulled her close. "So, who is your new friend?"

"Marla's date. They came in for a reading together. I have no idea where she is. She was glued to his side earlier."

Nick pressed his lips together to keep from laughing. "You really do have abominable luck sometimes."

"I do," Maddie agreed. "How was your day? Did ... did you find Cassidy?" She was almost afraid to ask.

Nick scowled. "I have searched for her everywhere. I swear she has to have left town or something. If she has, do you think that saves me from having to break up with her? I mean, if I never hear from her again, it's not really a relationship, is it?"

"You could always write her a note."

"Or an email."

"No one breaks up with someone via email."

"Some people do."

"Not good people," Maddie said.

Nick sighed. "You're right. I'm just ... so tired."

"It will get better, Nicky," Maddie said. "It can't get worse."

CASSIDY KEPT herself hidden in the shadows of the trees on the far side of the town square, her gaze focused squarely on Nick and Maddie as they twirled around the dance floor. They were laughing gaily, not a care in the world or an eye on anyone around them.

She'd thought if she hid from Nick he would feel guilty and rethink his decision. She'd thought he would be prostrate with worry while he looked for her. Instead, Nick looked happier fooling around with Maddie than he had ever looked when he was with her.

"It's disgraceful," Marla said, moving up next to Cassidy. "You're his girlfriend, and yet he's fawning all over Maddie. It's so disrespectful."

"It is," Cassidy agreed.

"You should do something about it."

"What?"

"Make sure Maddie Graves knows that she's poaching," Marla said. "Make sure she knows that you're aware of what she's doing. Make sure she knows that Nick is yours."

"And what if he's not?" Cassidy asked, her voice pitiful.

"Don't give her a choice," Marla said. "Nick is taken. If you don't put your foot down, you'll lose him forever. Maddie Graves needs to be put in her place, and I think you're just the person to do it."

11. ELEVEN

"I don't mean to interrupt, but I might have some interesting information," Christy said, sidling up to Nick and Maddie as they swayed on the dance floor.

Nick shot her a disapproving look. The last thing he wanted to do was move from his current position. "And what would that be?"

"Cassidy is here."

Nick froze, jerking his head around and scanning the crowd. "Where?"

"I saw her a few minutes ago," Christy said. "She was kind of hanging back. I don't think she wanted anyone to see her. She was talking to Marla."

"Well, that can't be good," Maddie said.

"No," Nick agreed. "Still ... if she's here ... I need to try and find her. If she disappears again, this could go on for days."

"Go," Maddie said, pulling away.

Nick immediately missed the feeling of her body against his. "I'll ... wait for me and I'll walk you home."

Maddie's face was rueful. "We both know you could have a long night ahead of you, and I'm tired. I think I'm going to head straight home."

"Are you sure?" Nick was disappointed.

"Nicky, this could take you all night, and I can't be involved in it," Maddie said.

"I know," Nick said, running his hand through his hair. "I still wish I could just send her an email."

"Classy," Christy snorted.

Nick glared at her. "Can I trust you to make sure Maddie makes it safely to her car without unwanted advances from Marla's friend?"

"Of course," Christy said. "I'll jump in front of him and beat my chest and tell him that if he touches her the local police detective will slap him silly."

Despite himself, Nick couldn't fight the grin as it spread across his face. "Thank you." He glanced at Maddie one more time. "I'll either see you tonight or tomorrow. I'm not sure which yet."

"Good luck."

Nick wanted to touch her. He wanted to kiss her, or at least give her a hug. He did neither. Instead, he gripped her shoulder for a moment and graced her with a small smile. "I'm going to need it."

"ARE you sure you don't want me to walk you to your car?" Christy asked.

Maddie waved off the offer. "I'll be fine." The duo had separated from Nick ten minutes before, and even though Christy was trying to entice Maddie with a few drinks, Maddie was too tired to even consider it. "You should stay here and have some fun."

"What fun?" Christy scoffed.

Maddie pointed toward a table about twenty feet away. "Isn't that Graham Snow?"

Christy followed Maddie's gaze. "Yeah. So what?"

"He's been watching you for half the night," Maddie said. "You should go and dance with him."

"Graham Snow is a ... ."

"Good-looking guy," Maddie finished. "You're too picky. Besides, no one says you have to marry him. A little dancing might do you good."

"So, why don't you do some dancing?" Christy challenged.

"I've already done some dancing," Maddie said. "The truth is, I just need some time alone to think."

"Because Nick is about to be free?"

"Because my feet hurt, and I'm exhausted," Maddie replied.

Christy waited, her face impatient.

"And I might want to think about Nick," Maddie conceded.

Christy grinned. "Well, as long as you promise to think dirty thoughts, I'll allow you to leave," she said. "Just ... be careful on your way to the car."

"What could possibly happen?" Maddie asked. "It's Blackstone Bay."

"Didn't two people try to kill you two weeks ago?"

Maddie scowled. "I see your point. Don't worry. It's still relatively early. I'll be fine."

"Just be careful," Christy said. "If something happens to you, Nick is going to burn this town down – and I'm going to help him."

"You say the sweetest things."

Maddie separated from Christy and pointed herself in the direction of home. She'd driven to the fair, but the parking lot was packed, and she didn't want to deal with traffic when she didn't have to. Her car would be fine in the parking lot overnight, and the evening was pleasant enough for Maddie to walk without working up too much of a sweat.

Since most of Blackstone Bay's denizens were down at the fair, even though midnight was approaching, the streets were quiet as Maddie traversed them. She took the opportunity to gaze up at the sky, studying the moon for hints. It was almost full. It felt like time was stalking Maddie – on more than one front – and she didn't know how to handle any of it.

The sound of footsteps echoing against pavement caught Maddie's attention, and she shifted. She'd opted to walk home barefoot. She hadn't been lying about the heels hurting too much to bear for another minute.

Maddie stilled her forward momentum and peered into the dark night, trying to zero in on a figure she knew was close. When the figure finally moved from the shadows across the road, Maddie recognized it instantly. Tara Warner. What was she doing out here alone?

Maddie studied her for a moment, conflicted. The woman's back was to her, and if she'd noticed Maddie walking on the opposite sidewalk, she wasn't showing any signs. Should she follow her? Should she let her go? Should she call Nick for help? Something told Maddie she didn't have a choice. She had to follow.

Maddie opened her mouth to yell to the woman. She had no idea what she was going to say, but the odds of someone approaching both Maddie and Tara were slim. Maddie could walk Tara to her destination. Maybe it would be enough to change the woman's destiny.

Maddie's greeting lodged in her throat when she saw another silhouette move about in the murky shadows. This one had detached from the small clump of trees in front of Sally's Bakery. Maddie hadn't even sensed another presence – not until it was too late. That was worrisome, but it was also a worry for another night.

Maddie wasn't sure what to do, but she knew the scene she'd witnessed a few nights before was about to happen. She couldn't change the vision then. That didn't mean she couldn't change it now.

The silhouette was behind Tara now, and the distance between the two figures was closing. Maddie took the opportunity to bolt across the street. The dark scarf Christy had secured on her head earlier hid some of her flaxen hair. She was still easy to spot, though, but since she was behind both Tara and her pursuer, she was going unnoticed.

Maddie's bare feet padded on the ground as she crossed, and the pavement radiated heat from earlier in the day. Maddie pushed it out of her mind, and once she was on the same sidewalk as Tara, she increased her pace.

The dark man – and it was a man, Maddie had no doubt – increased his pace as he moved in behind Tara. Maddie was still trailing, and she knew she was out of options when she saw the man's arm extend toward Tara's shoulder. Maddie flung one of the shoes she was carrying and it hit him square in the back before bouncing harmlessly to the ground.

He immediately stopped and swiveled so he was facing Maddie. Since he was wearing a dark hoodie – which was a dead giveaway in this heat – Maddie couldn't make out any features. Tara was still oblivious.

"Tara! Run!"

Tara froze when she heard the yell, pivoting quickly and looking behind her. She gasped when she saw the proximity of the man. "Maddie?"

"Run!"

"What the ... ?"

Maddie tossed her other shoe and hit the man in the head. He growled as it bounced off. It hadn't done any damage, but it felt good to throw it all the same. Instead of turning back to Tara, the man advanced on Maddie.

"Run!" Maddie repeated, taking a step back.

"Who is that?" Tara asked.

"I don't know," Maddie said. "I ... he was reaching for you."

"He's going after you now."

"I noticed." Maddie took another step backward, momentarily flapping her arms as she realized she was teetering on the edge of the curb before tumbling over. "Oh, crap."

"Maddie!" Tara jumped off of the sidewalk, giving the figure a wide berth as she circled around to help Maddie off the ground. Once side-by-side, Tara supporting half of Maddie's weight, the two women regarded the figure with fixed gazes. "What should we do?"

"I have no idea," Maddie said.

"Should we run?"

"I think he should run," Maddie said, an idea forming. "I called Nick right before I threw my shoes. I told him what was happening. He's on his way."

"Good," Tara said. "A police officer is exactly what we need."

The figure shifted his shoulders, uncertain. Finally, he took a step back and disappeared into the bushes that skirted a nearby house. He'd never said a word.

Once he was gone, Maddie finally allowed herself the opportunity to breathe.

"Did you really call Nick?" Tara asked, hopeful.

"No. You should call the police now, though. We have to report this."

"Are you okay?" Tara asked, studying Maddie worriedly.

Maddie sank back down to the cement and rubbed her ankle. "I think I twisted my ankle."

"Well ... thanks," Tara said, pulling her phone out of her purse. "I'm guessing this is what you saw when you read my cards the other day. This is what you didn't want to tell me, isn't it?"

Maddie balked. "I ... no ... I ... ."

"It's okay," Tara said. "I had a feeling you were hiding something. You put yourself in danger to protect me. I'm not going to tell anyone. Don't worry about it."

"Thank you," Maddie murmured.

"No. Thank you."

"SO, TELL ME WHAT HAPPENED AGAIN." Detective Dale Kreskin wasn't happy to be torn away from the festivities, even though he'd only had to walk three blocks when the call came in.

"I was walking home," Maddie said, still sitting on the pavement and rubbing her ankle. "I saw Tara on the sidewalk. I was about to call out to her, but then I saw some ... guy ... kind of sneak out of the trees over there."

"And what did you do?" Kreskin asked.

"I just kind of watched him for a second," Maddie said. "I wasn't sure if Tara knew him. Then I realized he was wearing a hoodie and his face was covered."

"And you found that suspicious?"

"It's still eighty-five degrees out," Maddie pointed out.

"Okay," Kreskin said, rubbing his chin. He'd obviously had a few drinks at the fair, which he was trying to hide. "So, what did he do then?"

"He kind of reached for her."

"And what did you do?"

"I threw my shoes at him."

Kreskin pressed his lips together to keep from laughing. "And then what happened?"

"I fell off the curb."

"And then?"

"I ... ."

"The guy was clearly up to no good," Tara said. "Who sneaks up on a woman when she's walking alone after dark?"

"Are you sure he wasn't just playing around?"

"If he was, it wasn't very funny."

"Okay," Kreskin said, giving in. "What do you think he wanted?"

Tara shrugged. "Maybe he wanted my purse."

"I guess that's a possibility," Kreskin conceded. "Did he say anything to either of you?"

"No."

"Did he have a weapon?"

"No."

"I just don't know what to do with this," Kreskin said. "There was no actual threat. How do I go after a guy who was walking on the sidewalk, who didn't say anything, and didn't try to hurt someone?"

"Should I have waited for him to slit her throat, or hit her on the head?" Maddie was getting angry.

"No," Kreskin said. "You should have done exactly what you did. Well, except for falling off the curb. That was a boneheaded move."

Maddie shot him a dark look.

"I'll file a report," Kreskin said. "That's all I can do."

"Well, great," Tara said.

Kreskin leaned down and grabbed Maddie under her arms and hoisted her to a standing position. "Come on. I'll carry you home and make sure Tara gets where she's supposed to be going. I think you should both take this as a sign that you shouldn't be wandering around after dark without an escort."

Maddie was incredulous. "You're going to carry me?"

"It's two blocks," Kreskin said. "I'd rather carry you than put up with the absolute fit Winters would pitch if I left you to your own devices. You need to put some ice on that ankle."

"My car is only a block away," Tara said.

"Then we'll walk past it on the way," Kreskin said, picking Maddie up and cradling her in his arms. "You two really know how to ruin a man's evening."

"I'd rather crawl home," Maddie announced.

"Yeah, Winters would love that," Kreskin said. "He'd beat me bloody. Now, shut your mouth. If I have to end my night early, you can at least be quiet.

"Oh, and when Nick asks about this, you tell him I was a perfect gentleman," he continued. "If he thinks my hands wandered even a millimeter, he's going to go nuclear – and no one wants that."

"Fine," Maddie conceded. "Mush. Mush."

Kreskin grinned. "I kind of like you. I have no idea why, but I do."

"I'm a likable person."

"You remind me of Maude," Kreskin said.

"That's the meanest thing anyone has ever said to me," Maddie replied.

"You'll live."

12. TWELVE

"Well, it looks better," Maude said, studying Maddie's ankle the next morning with a serious gaze. "The puffiness is gone. Is it still sore?"

"Kind of," Maddie admitted. "It's much better than it was last night, though."

"I don't know what you were thinking, Maddie girl, but that wasn't one of your smartest moves," Maude said.

"What was I supposed to do?"

"I don't know," Maude admitted. "I just know I don't like the idea of you going up against a strange man in the middle of the night. Something really bad could have happened."

"It was either that or let him grab Tara," Maddie said. "I couldn't live with that."

"I know," Maude said. "I just ... I happen to love you."

"Well, that's good. I happen to love you, too."

"You need to take better care of yourself," Maude said. "If you die now, I'm going to be very ticked off."

"Duly noted."

Maude's face relaxed. "What are you going to do today?"

"I have to go back and read tarot cards because you volunteered me for duty," Maddie reminded her.

"Well, you'll be sitting all day. That will probably be good for you."

"I'm only going to do readings for two hours," Maddie warned. "That's all I agreed to."

"I don't care," Maude said. "If I were you, I'd use the ankle as an excuse to make hot men carry me around on satin pillows all day."

Maddie snickered. "I'll consider it."

The two women looked up as Christy breezed into the room, her flame-red hair wild from rampant humidity. "Good morning, ladies."

"I like how you just let yourself in," Maddie said. "I should probably hide the key better. Nick just lets himself in, too."

"I think you're safe with Nick," Christy said, moving toward the counter so she could pour herself a mug of coffee. "So, I hear you took down an assailant with nothing but a pair of shoes last night."

Maddie balked. "Who told you?"

"You're the talk of the town," Christy said. "Everyone is talking about how you saved Tara – especially Tara."

"Oh, no." Maddie dropped her head into her hands. "What are they saying? Wait! I don't want to know."

"She didn't tell anyone anything bad," Christy said. "I'm assuming this had something to do with the vision you had about her, right?"

Maddie nodded, but she kept her face hidden.

"All Tara is telling people is that you noticed someone following her and intervened," Christy said. "You're a hero."

"I don't feel like a hero," Maddie said. "Is she also telling people how I fell off the curb and twisted my ankle?"

Christy grinned. "No. That does make the story more entertaining, though."

"It's not entertaining."

Christy glanced over at the ankle Maddie had propped up on a chair. "Does it hurt?"

"I iced it all night," Maddie said. "It feels better, although it's still tender."

"Well, don't worry. I'll drive you to the fair today," Christy said. "I'll make sure to bring you ice for it during the afternoon, too."

"You're a good friend," Maude said. "I'll come down and watch her later."

"You hate fairs," Maddie said.

"Yes, but I happen to love my granddaughter," Maude said. "Didn't we already go over this?"

Maddie scowled. "I'm fine. I'll make sure to leave the fair before it gets dark."

"I think Nick is going to be glued to your side for most of the day," Christy said. "Someone would have to be stupid to take him on to get to you. I'm surprised he's not here now."

Maddie was surprised by that non-development, too. "Have you seen Nick?" Maddie lifted her head. She was trying to feign mild interest, but her face was an open book.

Christy giggled. "No. I did hear a story about Cassidy running through the fair and jumping into her car a few minutes after you left, though. I don't think Nick got to have a conversation with her."

"That's just ... stupid," Maude said.

"Granny," Maddie scolded.

"I'm sorry. I feel for the girl. I do. This is just undignified, though."

"It is," Christy agreed. "Everyone in town is talking about it."

"I thought everyone in town was talking about me," Maddie said.

"When talk of Cassidy springs up, talk of you follows," Christy said pointedly. "Everyone knows Nick is trying to break up with her. Everyone."

"What are they saying about me?" Maddie asked, her voice small.

"They're saying they're surprised it's taken Nick this long to cut Cassidy loose," Christy said. "They've had a pool going. Most people picked the first week you got back for the breakup."

"You're joking, right?"

Christy shook her head. "I picked today in the pool," she said, her eyes sparkling. "I knew it would take you guys a little longer to get things together. I win five-hundred bucks if Nick pulls the plug today or tomorrow, so he really needs to get on that."

"Oh, I'm so embarrassed," Maddie said, miserable.

"You'll get over it," Christy said, patting Maddie's shoulders. "Now, if Nick hasn't found Cassidy by the end of the day, you need to tell me. I'll find her for him if it comes down to it. I want to splurge on some shoes."

"You're horrible," Maddie said, looking to her grandmother for support. "Tell her she's horrible."

"Hey, I had last week in the pool," Maude said. "You've already ruined things for me. Now I'm pulling for Christy."

Maddie was at a loss for words.

"Go upstairs and get showered and dressed," Christy said. "Call me up when you need your hair done."

"But ... ."

"Don't talk back to me," Christy said. "It's going to be a busy day, and I'm determined to be a rich woman before it's all said and done. I can't take any of your backtalk."

"I CAN'T BELIEVE how many people came in here this afternoon," Maddie said, focusing on Christy with a mixture of awe and exhaustion as she relaxed in her chair beneath the purple tent. "I just did fifty readings in four hours."

"I thought you were only going to do readings for two hours?"

"There was a line," Maddie said. "What was I supposed to do?"

"How much money did you make?"

"A lot."

"Enough to buy me some shoes if Nick fails?"

Maddie rolled her eyes. "Well, I'm done for the day. What do you want to do now?"

"Let's go to the fair."

"We're at the fair."

"I mean the carnival," Christy said. "We can get some junk food and people watch."

"People watch?"

"Hey, I like to people watch," Christy said. "It always gives me hope."

"Hope for what?"

"That I'm the coolest person in the world."

Maddie grinned. "I think you are."

"Oh, you're so sweet, Maddie. Do you want to change your clothes?"

Maddie nodded.

"I figured. Hurry up. I think we could both use some fun. We'll take it easy because of your ankle. I promise."

"WHAT'S OVER THERE?" Maddie asked, an elephant ear in one hand and a soda in the other. She loved junk food, and carnival food was king of the junk food hill.

"I don't know," Christy said. "Let's look."

The two women shuffled over toward a crowd of hooting-and-hollering people, Maddie still limping slightly. When they pushed their way to the front, Maddie couldn't hide the smile from her face.

"Oh, it's the dunk tank," Christy said. "I'd forgotten about this."

"What's the charity this year?"

"The Blackstone Bay Pet Rescue Society."

"Oh, well, that's a good charity," Maddie said, her eyes sparkling as they focused on the man sitting in the dunk tank. He was taunting a group of young boys as they lobbed balls at the target – not one of them getting close enough to put him in danger.

"Are you going to buy some balls to dunk him?"

"I am."

Christy smirked. "Well, that will be fun. The faster you dunk Nick, the faster he can put someone else in there and get on task. I need some new shoes."

Maddie giggled. "I just want him to be at my mercy."

"Oh, girl, he's been at your mercy for as long as I can remember."

NICK DIDN'T IMMEDIATELY NOTICE Maddie's presence. He was having fun messing with the Baker brothers. They were little delinquents in training, and neither one of them had a strong enough arm to hit the target.

After a few moments, he scanned the crowd, and his gaze immediately landed on Maddie. She was dressed in simple cutoffs and a T-shirt, and her hair was piled high on the back of her head in a messy bun, but she took his breath away.

"Hey, Officer Winters," Christy teased, handing a five-dollar bill over to the cashier by the table and collecting three softballs. "How are you this fine, hot day?"

Nick glowered at Christy. "Aren't you a bit old for this?"

"I'm young at heart." Christy threw the first ball and missed by a good three feet.

"You were never much of an athlete, were you?" Nick was feeling relatively safe, despite Christy's determination.

Christy glowered at him and threw another ball. This one was closer, but it didn't hit the target. "You're awfully full of yourself."

Nick winked at Maddie. "That's because I know you can't hit a small target with one of those balls."

"Oh, really?"

"Really."

Christy concentrated and tossed her final ball, frowning as it sailed wide. "Darn it."

Maddie patted her shoulder. "It's okay."

"Well, you promised to let me go first," Christy said. "Have at it."

Nick froze in his spot. "Excuse me?"

"It's Maddie's turn," Christy said, smiling evilly. "She wanted to go first, but I convinced her my need was more dire. It turns out, I'm a horrible shot. Something tells me she's going to be better at it."

Something told Nick that Christy was right. While she was never on any organized teams, Maddie had always been an outstanding athlete. It probably had something to do with the fact that she was always running around in the woods with him.

"Now, Mad, think about this," Nick said. "You don't really want me to get all wet, do you?"

Maddie collected her balls and handed over her money, her face apologetic but pleased. "It's a hot day, Nicky. Your face is red. I think you've been sitting out in the sun too long. It will probably do you good to cool off."

"Mad ... wait."

Maddie threw the first ball, only missing the target by an inch and drawing a loud groan from the crowd.

Nick flinched as he gripped the wooden plank beneath him. "Now, Mad, you've had your fun. How about we call it a draw and I'll buy you some ice-cream?"

"Yeah, Maddie," someone in the crowd yelled. "He'll buy you some ice-cream if you let him keep his dignity."

Maddie faltered. Nick's face was unreadable when she lifted her eyes to his. "You know I have to do this, Nicky."

"Why do you have to do it?"

"It's your payback for scaring me the other night."

Nick wrinkled his nose. "That was an accident. This is on purpose."

"Oh, how did he scare you?" Someone else asked. "Did he take his pants off?"

This drew guffaws from the crowd. Maddie took advantage of the momentary confusion and lobbed the second ball. This one ticked the side of the target, but it wasn't with enough force to drop Nick into the water.

He exhaled heavily. "Just know, when I get out of here, I'm going to make you pay," he warned.

"I know," Maddie said. "I just can't stop myself." The third ball hit the target a second later, and Nick's face was resigned as he dropped into the water.

The crowd broke into enthusiastic applause as Nick surfaced. He brushed the water away from his face and climbed out of the tank, watching momentarily as Kreskin climbed in after him. "She's a beast," Kreskin said. "I'm glad she's your problem and not mine."

"Me, too," Nick said, grabbing a towel and rubbing it over his hair as he watched the townspeople congratulate an embarrassed Maddie. She looked happy. "Me, too."

13. THIRTEEN

"I suppose you think that was funny." Nick was watching Maddie as he dried off. Her grin was so wide he couldn't look away. It was like looking into the sun, but not getting burned.

"I don't know if funny is the right word," Maddie hedged, pushing Nick's sopping hair out of his face.

"What word would you use?"

"Relaxing."

Nick shook his head, but couldn't help but smile. Maddie was practically giddy. "Well, you'd better hold on to that feeling," he said. "Because I'm probably going to ruin your mood for a few minutes."

Maddie's face slackened, and Nick immediately wanted to pull the words back into his mouth. "Why? Did something happen?"

"Don't freak out, Mad," Nick said. "I was referring to last night."

"Oh."

"Oh." Nick nodded. "Is there a reason I had to hear about your little adventure from Dale Kreskin?"

"I didn't want to bother you." Maddie dropped her head. "I knew you were busy."

"I wasn't as busy as I would have liked," Nick said. "That doesn't mean you shouldn't have called me." He reached over and tipped her chin up. "When you're in trouble, Mad, I want to be there."

"I know," Maddie said. "I just ... ."

"I'm not mad," Nick said, sighing. "I am worried." He glanced around to make sure no one was eavesdropping. "Did you save her for good? Was that what you saw in your dream?"

"It was what I saw. I don't know if that was the end, though."

Nick cupped the back of Maddie's neck and rubbed it thoughtfully. "Well, we'll take it one step at a time. I heard you hurt your ankle. Is that why you're limping?"

"It's better than it was."

"Well, you should still keep off of it as much as possible."

"Thank you, doctor."

Nick pinched her neck playfully. "Well, I need to get out of these clothes."

"I'm pretty sure I can't help you with that," Maddie said. "I didn't realize you were that kind of doctor."

"You're cute."

Maddie's smile twisted his heart. "Thank you."

"I have a change of clothes back at the station," he said. "If you promise to sit here and rest, I'll be back in fifteen minutes. I'll buy you that ice-cream I promised."

"You promised me ice-cream if I didn't dunk you."

"Yeah, well, I'm a softy," Nick said. "I'll also buy you an elephant ear and an icee."

"And then will you hold my hair back while I puke from all that junk?"

"Yes." Nick didn't miss a beat. "I'll also win you a huge stuffed animal if you watch me play a few games."

"You always did like playing the games."

"Only so I could win you prizes," Nick said.

"How about we compromise?"

Nick arched an eyebrow and waited.

"How about I go and look at the flea market stands while you change your clothes and you find me there?"

"Should you be walking on that ankle, Mad?"

"Are you going to carry me around all night, Nicky?"

"I just might."

Maddie rolled her eyes. "It's much better than it was. It's not like I'll be running."

Nick glanced over her shoulder and studied the flea market tables for a moment. "Okay. I'll agree to your terms if you're careful."

"Do you think someone is going to try and grab me while it's still daylight out?"

"Well, you're awfully pretty," Nick teased. "Some men may not be able to help themselves."

Maddie's cheeks burned under the praise. "I ... ."

"It was just a compliment, Mad," Nick said. "There's no reason to hang your head in shame." He gave her a quick kiss on the forehead. "Don't spend too much money at the flea market. If I have to carry huge bags around, it's going to weigh me down."

"I'll keep that in mind."

"You do that."

MADDIE HAD ALWAYS LOVED a flea market. Every table was a new realm to explore, and the treasures hidden there were varied. While she waited for Nick to return, she moved from table to table and perused the various trinkets. She bought a pair of earrings for Christy, and a necklace for Maude, and then stopped at a small table that made stone statues out of Petoskey stones.

That's where Nick found her ten minutes later. "I see you've already been buying things."

"I have," Maddie said, picking up one of the small statues and handing it to the woman behind the counter. "How much?"

"Five dollars."

Maddie paid the woman and took the statue back, handing it to Nick with bright eyes. "For luck."

Nick looked the statue over, confused. "Is this a turtle made out of Petoskey stones?"

"Yes."

"You bought this for me?"

"It just reminded me of you," Maddie said. "I always give you Petoskey stones for luck, and you always catch turtles for me so I can name them and release them. I just thought ... oh ... it's stupid. Never mind. You don't have to keep it."

Nick clasped his hand around the tiny statue and jerked it away when Maddie tried to retrieve her gift. "You can't take it back. That's not how you give a present."

"But ... you don't like it."

"Did I say I didn't like it?"

"No."

"Then don't put words in my mouth," Nick said. "I happen to love it."

"I think you're just saying that to make me feel better," Maddie said.

"I don't really care what you think," Nick teased, slipping the statue into his pocket. "I happen to think this is the best gift anyone has ever given me, and you can't take it back."

"You're incorrigible sometimes."

"I am," Nick agreed. He held his hand out. "Let's go to the fair."

Maddie studied his outstretched hand a moment, unsure.

"Do I have cooties now?"

"I don't think we should do that in public right now," Maddie said, worrying her bottom lip with her teeth.

"Hold hands? Is that suddenly against the law? You would think someone would have told me." Nick dropped his hand, slightly hurt by her refusal to touch him.

"It's just that ... did you know they have a pool?"

"I don't think anyone in town has a pool," Nick said. "We have lakes and rivers. We don't need pools."

"Not that kind of pool," Maddie snapped. "They have a pool for when you're going to break up with Cassidy."

Realization dawned on Nick, and he fought the mad urge to laugh. "No. That's funny, though."

"They're all waiting and watching us."

"Why do you think they're watching us?" Nick asked pointedly.

He knew exactly why the townspeople were watching them, but he was curious whether Maddie would admit it or not.

"I ... I don't want to talk about that until ... ."

"Okay," Nick conceded.

"It just doesn't seem right."

"I understand, Mad," Nick said. "We won't talk about it yet. Just so you know, though, we are going to be having a very serious discussion in the near future, so you'd better be ready."

"I'm ready."

Nick snorted. "You don't look ready. We don't have to worry about that tonight. You don't have to hold my hand, and you don't have to worry about people talking about us."

"Are you suddenly magic?"

"I'm always magic," Nick said, sweeping his arm out grandiosely. "Milady, shall we go to the fair and proceed not to touch each other all night?"

"Oh, you think you're so cute," Maddie grumbled.

"I'm handsome, not cute," Nick said. "Get it right."

"Well, Officer Handsome, I'm hungry."

"Well, we can't have that," Nick said. "What do you want first?"

"A hot dog."

"Oh, good, health food."

"**DO** you want me to try and throw the ball through the hoop?"

Nick scowled. "I can do it. I promised I was going to win you a stuffed animal, and I meant it."

"You've dropped twenty bucks." Maddie was enjoying herself. She didn't care about the stuffed animal, and she didn't care about the game, but she was having a great time watching Nick struggle. He was always the best at everything. It was nice to see him grapple with failure – however small – for a change.

"Shh."

Nick tossed the ball and missed again. "Sonovabitch!"

Maddie pressed her lips together to keep from laughing. "Here."

She put a ten-dollar bill on the counter and motioned for the man running the game to hand her some balls. "How many do I have to get in?"

"Two out of three," he said. "If you get three, you can get one of the big animals up there."

Maddie glanced where he was pointing. "Even the turtle?"

"Even the turtle."

"Are we having a turtle theme tonight?" Nick asked.

"Shh. I'm concentrating."

Nick rolled his eyes, but he took a step back so Maddie could focus on her task. The first ball she tossed flew through the hoop easily. The second tipped the side but ultimately fell through. The third was perfect.

"We have a winner!" The game master reached up and snagged the turtle. "Here you go, ma'am."

"Thank you," Maddie said, taking the turtle.

"This doesn't count," Nick said. "I wanted to win you a stuffed animal. Me."

"Well, I'm going to name this one Nick," Maddie said, grinning. "And I don't even have to throw him back." The double meaning registered on Maddie, and she was instantly embarrassed. "I didn't mean ... ."

"Yes, you did," Nick said. "Don't you dare take it back." He grabbed the stuffed animal from her and held it up so he could see it better. "This looks nothing like me. Still, if you promise to sleep with it every night, I'll pretend I won it for you and we'll both be happy."

Maddie's eyes were wide as he glanced back at her. "I have a feeling our talk is going to take days, Mad," he said.

"You said ... ."

"We're not talking about it tonight," he said. "We're not talking and we're not touching. Where to next?"

Maddie scanned the fair. "I could use an icee."

"Let's go."

"I don't think you're having fun," Maddie said. "I think you'd rather be doing something else."

"That's not true, Mad," Nick said. "I wouldn't want to be anywhere else. I just feel like I should be doing something else so we have one less worry on our shoulders."

"Cassidy," Maddie said, falling into step next to him. "Christy said she was seen running to her car and speeding away last night."

"Yup. I got one look at her and she bolted," Nick said. "I feel like an idiot. If I'd gotten to her last night, who would have won the pool?"

"I have no idea," Maddie said. "I just know if you finish your task tonight, or tomorrow, Christy wins five-hundred bucks. She's going to buy shoes."

Nick chuckled. "Well, at least Cassidy's heartbreak will go to a good cause."

"I feel bad for her," Maddie said. "I feel ... guilty."

"Don't," Nick said. "She's doing it to herself now. Everyone in this stinking town knows what's going to happen. So, instead of dealing with it, she's hiding like a child. I just ... I had no idea she would act this way."

"Maybe that's your super power," Maddie suggested.

"What?"

"You have the power to make smart women go insane," she said. "You're ... Tortured Love Man."

Nick burst out into hysterical laughter. "I had never considered that." He wiped a tear from his eye. "That's not my only super power, though, Mad."

"Oh, really? What's the other?"

"I can't show you until after our talk."

Maddie's face colored again. "You are just so full of yourself."

"I am," Nick said. "Come on. You need an icee. How about, after that, we go to the funhouse. We haven't been to one of those in a very long time."

"Not since the summer before I left for college," Maddie said, rueful.

"I remember," Nick said. "You got scared and threw yourself on me. It was the first time I realized you had such big boobs, because they were crushed against my chest. It was the best thirty seconds of my life – up until then, of course."

Maddie's mouth dropped open. "I can't believe you just said that to me."

"I know. I'm a horrible person. You should spank me later."

"You're just getting worse and worse," Maddie said.

"I'm trying. Come on. One icee coming up, and then I'm going to hope you get so scared in the funhouse you forget your mandate about touching."

"Oh, you *are* Tortured Love Man," Maddie said.

"I'll get a cape."

14. FOURTEEN

"I'll be right back," Nick said, reluctantly getting up from the table he and Maddie were sitting at. "Finish your icee."

"Where are you going?" Maddie asked, confused.

Nick pointed to the beer tent, where Ted Potter and Alan Kocis were getting ready to throw punches. "Don't worry. If I distract them for a few minutes, they'll forget what they were fighting about."

"Well, that sounds ... fun."

"Drink your icee and rest your ankle," Nick instructed. "I've noticed you limping more and more as the night progresses. That means you're sore. You're going to need all your strength not to touch me in the funhouse. I'll try to help you with your struggle, but there's only so much I can do. I really am irresistible."

Maddie rolled her eyes, smiling as he walked away. After a few minutes of watching him try to talk Ted and Alan down, she let her eyes drift. That's when her gaze fell on Cassidy. She was standing about fifty yards away, well out of Nick's sight line, and she was staring at Maddie from the edge of the fairgrounds.

Maddie kept her eyes on the woman, unsure of what to do. If she alerted Nick, not only would she make a scene, but Cassidy was likely to bolt. The last thing she wanted was a scene. Without breaking eye contact, Maddie got to her feet and headed in Cassidy's direction. She left the turtle to save her spot, and as a message for Nick that she wouldn't be gone long.

Cassidy waited for Maddie to close the distance, and then she stepped farther back so she was hidden underneath the canopy of trees that skirted the fair area. When Maddie joined her there, Cassidy's face was like stone.

"People have been looking for you," Maddie said, hoping her voice was free of recrimination.

"You mean Nick has been looking for me," Cassidy corrected.

"Last time I checked, Nick was a person," Maddie said. "Has that changed when I wasn't looking?"

"Oh, so much has changed since you came back to this town I've lost track," Cassidy said. "You know you've ruined my life, right?"

"I didn't ruin your life," Maddie said, trying to remain calm. "I came home to live my life. You're the one ruining your life. Good grief, Cassidy, everyone in this town is talking about what you're doing.

"People saw you run at the dance last night," she continued. "They saw you run so you wouldn't have to talk to Nick. It's just so ... ."

"What? Immature?"

"I didn't say that," Maddie said.

"You were thinking it," Cassidy sneered.

She had been thinking it, but Maddie let it slide. "What do you hope to accomplish by doing this?"

"I don't know," Cassidy said, her voice shrill. "I keep thinking that this will all pass. I keep thinking that Nick will come to his senses and realize that he loves me. I keep thinking he'll finally look at you and see you for what you really are."

"And what's that?"

"A whore," Cassidy said coldly. "You're a whore who abandoned your best friend because you thought you were going to be something great. Then, when you failed in the real world, you came back here with your tail between your legs and tried to take back what you'd lost."

Maddie wanted to argue, but from Cassidy's point-of-view, that sounded exactly like what she'd done. There was no way Maddie could tell her the truth, so she let the woman have her pride and misguided notions. "I'm sorry my return has cast your life into upheaval."

"Oh, will you listen to yourself? You're just so full of it."

"What do you want me to say, Cassidy?"

"I want you to admit that you've somehow tricked Nick into wanting to break up with me."

"I haven't," Maddie said, standing firm. "Nick's decisions are his, and his alone."

"Then how come we were happy until you came back to town? How come we were planning for a future? How come we were talking about moving in together?"

Maddie faltered. Nick hadn't told her any of those things. "I ... ."

"Oh, you don't have anything to say now? Well, that's just great," Cassidy snapped. "Do you have any idea what you've done to me? You've stolen the man I love. You've confused him. Now he's going to just throw me away because ten years of pining for you have turned him into an emotional cripple."

"I understand you want to blame me," Maddie said. "I don't know what I would do if I was in your position."

"Oh, well, great," Cassidy said. "Thanks for your support."

Maddie ignored the sarcasm. "I do know what I wouldn't do, though. I wouldn't have run away from my house in the middle of the night to avoid a breakup. I wouldn't have hidden for days because I couldn't face talking to someone. And I certainly wouldn't have caused a scene in front of the townspeople who Nick has sworn to protect as a police officer."

Cassidy ran her tongue over her teeth, considering. "Do you think I'm proud of my actions?"

"No. I think you're embarrassed. I also think you just keeping making things worse."

"Oh, that's easy for you to say, isn't it?" Cassidy charged. "You're out on a date with my boyfriend. Life is just great for you. I mean, he's bought you a hot dog, and an elephant ear, and an icee. He's even won you a stupid turtle. Your life is great."

Maddie furrowed her brow, concerned. "Have you been following us?"

"No," Cassidy said, scandalized. "I just ... ."

"You've been watching us." Maddie was alarmed. She'd known Cassidy was unbalanced, but spying was just so ... wrong. "Why?"

"You know why," Cassidy said. "The only way I can see my own boyfriend is to hide in the shadows and watch him fawn all over you."

"Cassidy, I don't want to be involved with this," Maddie said. "Your relationship with Nick is your own."

"How can you even stand there and say something like that to me?" Cassidy asked, incensed. "My relationship with Nick changed irrevocably the second he laid eyes on you. The second. He didn't want anything to do with me after that. He acted like I was a burden."

"I don't think Nick is particularly proud of his actions," Maddie said. "You have to understand, we had some things to work out."

"You mean how you just abandoned him and left him in the dirt?"

"That's not what happened," Maddie said, annoyed. "You can't speak about things you don't understand. What happened back then was ... a mistake. I've always regretted it. You don't know what you're talking about."

"I know you didn't pick up a phone for ten years," Cassidy charged.

"No, I didn't," Maddie agreed. "Nick suffered because of my actions. I suffered, too. He's the best friend I've ever had."

"You don't want to be just friends, though, do you?"

Maddie swallowed her upper lip with her lower. This was not a conversation she ever wanted to have with Cassidy. "I don't know what's going to happen down the road." That wasn't a lie. It also wasn't the answer Cassidy was seeking.

"I see the way Nick looks at you," Cassidy said. "That's all I've been seeing for weeks. How do you think it made me feel to go out to dinner with my boyfriend, the first date we'd had in more than a week because he was so busy, mind you, and have him suggest I go home with another man so he could protect you?"

"I ... not good."

"No, not good," Cassidy agreed. "My boyfriend was willing to let me go home with a murderer because he was desperate to be with you."

"Okay, you're upset. I get it, and I accept it. Let's not go over the edge, though. It's not like Nick realized Todd was a murderer then."

"Oh, no, you're right," Cassidy said. "I'd hate to talk bad about my boyfriend with his mistress."

"Now you wait just a second," Maddie said. "We haven't done anything."

"He's spent the night at your house."

"And nothing has happened."

"I don't believe you."

"I can't fix that," Maddie said. "The truth is, your fight isn't with me. It's with Nick. You won't talk to him, though. Instead, you're lurking in the shadows like some sort of crazy stalker and dodging him in the hopes that ... what ... he'll somehow change his mind? You're only reinforcing his decision.

"Do you know how embarrassed he is by this turn of events?" Maddie continued. "The people in town are laughing. And, while they find Nick's part in this amusing, they're not just laughing at him. They're making a joke of you, too. Is that what you want?"

"Don't you dare talk to me about what I want," Cassidy said, extending a shaking finger in Maddie's direction. "What I want is for you to leave town. What I want is my boyfriend back. What I want is my life back."

"You have a life, Cassidy," Maddie said. "It shouldn't revolve around me, though."

Cassidy let loose with an exasperated sigh. "You're not even sorry, are you?"

"I'm sorry you're hurting so badly," Maddie said. "I'm sorry you're so unhappy. I'm not sorry for coming home, though. I'm not sorry for patching things up with Nick. I'm not sorry for being able to spend time with my grandmother. I will never be sorry for those things."

"Are you sorry for stealing my boyfriend?"

"I didn't steal your boyfriend," Maddie said. "You drove him away."

Cassidy's face fell, and her lower lip started to tremble. "No. It's your fault."

"As long as you keep telling yourself that, you'll never be able to move on."

"Oh, I'm not moving on," Cassidy said, pulling herself together. "I'm just here to give you a message. Nick Winters is my boyfriend. He's mine. You can't have him. I'm never going to give him to you."

"I think you should be talking with Nick about this," Maddie said, weary.

"I think you're right," Cassidy said, turning on her heel and stalking in the opposite direction of the fair.

"Nick's the other way," Maddie said.

"I'm not talking to Nick here," Cassidy scoffed. "That's what you want, and I'm never going to give you what you want."

Once Cassidy was gone, Maddie leaned against the closest tree so she could collect herself. That was one conversation she hoped she would never have to engage in. She felt emotionally dirty. Cassidy's thinking was convoluted, but Maddie couldn't help but wonder if she wouldn't be just as bitter if she was in the sad woman's shoes.

Maddie pinched the bridge of her nose to ward off an oncoming headache and shifted when she heard the crackle of underbrush beneath the canopy. Great. Was Cassidy coming back for round two?

When Maddie shifted, the air fled her lungs. The figure standing at the edge of the trees had come from the direction of the football field, not town. It was tall, and dark ... and wearing a hoodie.

"Oh, crud," Maddie muttered, taking a step back and smacking her head against the trunk of the tree. "You can't be serious. You can't think you're going to take me from here."

The man didn't say anything. Instead, he took a step forward. Maddie skirted around the tree, being careful not to rest too much weight on her sore ankle, and shuffled backward. "You're a ballsy little jerk," she said. "It takes guts to come after me when there are hundreds of people on the other side of those trees."

Still nothing. He took another step forward. In her haste to take large step back, Maddie planted her foot a little too hard and her injured ankle screamed in protest. "Oh!" Maddie tumbled backward inadvertently, falling for the second time in twenty-four hours. She was nothing if not graceful.

This time, the man increased his pace as he approached. Maddie knew she was out of options, so she opened her mouth – and let loose with a blood-curdling scream that could wake the dead. "Nick!"

15. FIFTEEN

Nick had just about calmed Ted and Alan down, and he was directing them back toward the bar when a scream pierced the humid air.

"Nick!"

He jerked his head, his gaze landing on the spot he'd left Maddie several minutes before, and then he broke into a run. She wasn't at the table, and she was screaming for him. Where was she?

Nick tore into the mass of trees, pulling up short when he saw her. She was on the ground nursing her ankle, and her shoulders were shaking. He scanned the trees, but she appeared to be alone. "Maddie?" He moved to her side and dropped to his knees. "Did you hurt your ankle?"

"I ... there was someone here," Maddie said, gasping. "He was wearing a hoodie. He started after me. I was trying to get away when I fell again. I'm a total klutz."

"Where?"

Maddie pointed in the direction of the football field. Nick moved to the trees and gazed out, searching for a hint of movement. After a few minutes, he returned to Maddie's side. "There's no one there."

"I ... he was here."

"Okay," Nick said, holding up his hands. "I believe you."

Maddie pressed the heel of her hand against her forehead. "I ... I just screamed. I'm sorry. I didn't know what else to do."

"You did the right thing, Mad," Nick said, reaching underneath her legs and pulling her to his lap. "You're okay, right? Other than your ankle, I mean."

"I'm fine."

Her face said otherwise. "You scared the life out of me," he said. "Why were you over here?"

"I ... saw Cassidy."

"You're kidding." Nick looked around again. "Where?"

"Right here."

"Why didn't you tell me?"

"I didn't want to make a scene," Maddie replied. "I think she was here to talk to me."

"What did she say?"

"She said I've ruined her life."

"Don't blame yourself, Mad."

"She said you two were going to move in together until I showed up." Maddie averted her eyes from Nick's piercing gaze.

"That's not true, Mad. You know that's not true. Don't let her get to you."

"She's really angry, Nicky. I don't blame her. From her perspective, I ruined your life when I left, and then I ruined her life when I came back."

"You did ruin my life when you left," Nick said. "You also saved it when you came back. I'm sorry for whatever she said to you."

"It's not your fault. She's just really sad."

"Well, she's going to have to deal," Nick said, struggling to get to his feet and still maintain Maddie's weight in his arms. "I'm done playing this game. I'm going to take you home, and then I'm not stopping until I find her. You could have been seriously hurt."

"There's no way she could've known about our ... friend."

"Are you sure?"

"I'm sure," Maddie said. "Cassidy is mixed up, but she's not mean."

"Well, I'm going to unmix things," Nick said. "You're going home and straight to bed. We'll pick up your turtle on the way."

"She says she's going to keep you," Maddie warned.

"Where she's concerned, I'm already gone, Mad. She's just going to have to deal with it."

AFTER THREE HOURS of fruitless searching, Nick was at his wit's end. He'd considered returning to Maddie's house, the need to be near her overwhelming, but he tempered his urges. She needed her sleep, and he had to deal with Cassidy.

Nick let himself into his house, dropping the keys on the table by the front door and slamming the deadbolt into place behind him. Before he could reach for the light switch, the overhead lamp in the living room flared to life.

Nick inadvertently jumped, and when he saw who was standing at the edge of the room, he internally sighed. Cassidy had gone all out. She was wearing a red lace teddy that pumped her breasts up to unnatural heights, and garter belts that left little to the imagination below the belt. Her hair was blown out, and she was standing next to his recliner watching him.

"It's about time you came home," she said.

Nick licked his lips. "How did you get in my house?"

"You left the back door unlocked."

Nick knew that was a lie. He never left the door unlocked. He glanced over her shoulder, the unmistakable signs of a missing pane of glass in the back door catching his attention. He'd deal with that later. It was the least of his worries now. "I've been looking for you."

"Well, I'm right here," Cassidy said, flouncing around the chair and moving toward him.

Nick purposely shuffled to the other side of the coffee table to cut her off. "We need to talk."

"Later," Cassidy said. "We can talk later. There are other things I want to do now."

"We're going to talk now."

"Oh, don't be such a fuddy-duddy," Cassidy said, reaching over so she could run her finger up his chest.

Nick grabbed her finger firmly. "Just so there aren't any misunderstandings, we're over."

Cassidy flinched. "What do you mean?"

"I don't know if you've lost your mind, or if you're playing a game, or if you're just ... freaking out ... but we're done. This relationship has been over for weeks, you just wouldn't accept it. I'm saying it now, though. We're through."

"You don't mean that," Cassidy said, jerking her hand back. "You're just confused."

"I'm not confused. I don't want to be with you."

"You do."

"Cassidy, in case you haven't noticed, we haven't been together in two months."

"Since Maddie came home," Cassidy spat.

"Have you been paying attention? I was separating myself from you two weeks before Maddie came back to town."

Cassidy faltered. "That's not true."

"It is true. Come on, Cassidy. I know you heard the rumors about me before we started dating. Everyone knew my schedule. Six months. That was all I was equipped for. I didn't want a serious relationship.

"You knew that going in," Nick continued. "I never let you stay here in the entire six months we were dating. I never spent more than two nights a week with you. That was by design. It shouldn't have been a surprise for you when the time started ticking down to goodbye."

"But ... we were happy."

Nick was at a loss. "I wasn't happy."

Cassidy reared back as if she'd been struck. "You were so."

"I was ... settled ... kind of. I wasn't going out and cheating on you, but I knew there was no future for us. I'm sorry you seem to think there was. That was not my intention."

"We had a future ahead of us," Cassidy countered. "I had a plan.

On our one-year anniversary, you were going to propose. Six months after that, we were going to get married in a nice outdoor ceremony. Two years after that we were going to have our first child."

She was delusional. There could be no other explanation. "You weren't going to last past the six-month mark."

"We've been dating seven months," Cassidy pointed out.

"Because I didn't want to rock the boat."

"What? I don't understand."

"We had a murder in town, and ... there was other stuff going on. I didn't want to deal with a breakup when I had so much else going on."

"So, you're saying you couldn't be bothered to break up with me?"

When she put it like that ... . Shame flooded through Nick. "Sadly, yes."

"And I suppose you're going to tell me that this has nothing to do with Maddie."

Nick rubbed the back of his neck as he sank down on the couch. "I can't tell you that."

"See. I knew she'd been working you. She denied it."

"She hasn't been working me," Nick said. "In fact, she's been fighting me off until I could deal with you. My disinterest in you really doesn't have anything to do with Maddie, at least not in the way you think it does."

"I don't believe you."

"Sit down, Cassidy," Nick ordered.

Cassidy started moving toward him.

"In the chair."

She scowled, but she settled there anyway.

"There are some things we need to talk about," Nick said. "First off, I am very sorry for the way I've treated you. It hasn't been fair. It hasn't been nice. It hasn't been ... tolerable. I've treated you very poorly, and I'll always feel bad for it."

"We can still work through it," Cassidy said, desperate. "We're not lost yet."

Nick held up his hand to stifle her. "I'm not breaking up with you because Maddie came home," he said. "I *am* breaking up with you because of Maddie, though."

Nick rested his hands on his knees, rubbing them against his jeans as he geared up for some long-coming truth. "I've been in love with Maddie since I was seventeen years old."

"Puppy love," Cassidy said. "You've just elevated it in your mind."

"No," Nick said, shaking his head. "What Maddie and I share is ... beyond anything I've ever felt for anyone. She almost broke me when she left, and then she did break me when she cut off contact."

"And yet you still love her."

"She had reasons for what she did," Nick said. "I'm not sharing them with you, and I'm not pretending her reasons were right. She made a mistake. She knows it. She'll always be sorry. She can't erase ten years of misery, but we can move forward. I'm beyond her leaving now. I don't want to dwell on it. She's home."

"And you're going to be with her, aren't you?"

"I am."

"Are you going to break up with her in six months, too? Is she aware of your *schedule*?" Cassidy was bitter, and she was almost at her breaking point.

"I didn't have a six-month schedule simply because I didn't want to get close to someone," Nick said. "I had it because I didn't want to get close to anyone but her. I know it sounds crazy, and simple, and little sad, but I was always waiting for *her*."

"How did you know she would come back?"

"Because I had faith," Nick replied. "I had faith that we belonged together and that we would find our way back to each other when the time was right. I was willing to wait forever for her if it came to it."

"And you didn't care who you hurt in the process, did you?"

"I cared," Nick said. "I just didn't let myself think about it too much. What I've done to you is unforgivable. I don't expect some happy hug and well wishes. I know you've been hurt, and I know you're going to keep hurting. I can't fix that."

"You're willing to break me like she broke you, though."

"There are three people in our little triangle," Nick said. "If I stay with you, you'll be happy and everyone else will be miserable."

"So, you're sacrificing me for Maddie's happiness?"

"If that's the way you want to look at it. The truth is, I'm ready to be happy. I can't be happy with you. She's all I've ever wanted. She's all I'll ever want. I'm very sorry that you got caught up in all of this. You'll never know how sorry I am. I know that doesn't help you. I know it doesn't make you feel any better. I just ... I need her."

Cassidy's face crumbled. "You can't believe that she's a better girlfriend than I am."

"That's neither here nor there. There's no such thing as a better girlfriend. There's just love. She's my whole heart, and nothing is ever going to change that. The thing you need to understand, though, is that even without Maddie in the picture, I never would be able to love you."

Cassidy was openly sobbing now.

"There are times in life when you know where you belong," Nick said, his heart twisting as he watched Cassidy convulse with body-wracking sobs. "I have always known I belonged with Maddie. I hope there's a day in the future – and I hope it's soon – where you find someone to belong with."

"I did."

"No, you didn't," Nick said, sympathy rolling off of him. "You only thought you did. When it really happens, you won't have to change who you are to fit into a little box. That's what you tried to do with me. That's not love."

"I'm going to be the laughingstock of this town." Cassidy's face was shifting. She was no longer sad. Now she was vengeful. "Everyone is going to laugh at me, and you're going to have your happy ending with Maddie. How is that fair?"

"Life isn't fair," Nick said. "I can't fix this for you, though. I'm sorry you're hurt, and I'm sorry you're embarrassed, but you did bring a lot of this on yourself. Your actions over the past few days have been ... unbelievable."

"So, this is my fault?"

"No," Nick said, holding firm. "You can blame this all on me. Tell everyone you need to that I'm a horrible person. I don't deny it. I just need this to be done."

"Well, bully for you," Cassidy snapped, getting to her feet. "We're done. Go and get your happy ending. Don't expect me to be waiting when she dumps you in the dirt again."

"I understand." Nick wasn't about to engage in another argument.

Cassidy strode toward the back door, grabbing her coat off the kitchen table as she navigated through the house. "You're going to regret this."

"I hope you find some happiness, Cassidy. I really do."

16. SIXTEEN

Nick was in the middle of an extraordinary dream when he suddenly lost the ability to breathe. He jerked awake to find a woman sitting on the edge of his bed. It wasn't the blonde one he'd been dreaming about, though.

"Mom."

"Good morning, Nick." Sharon Winters was a kind woman, but she was clearly enjoying her son's discomfort. She was in her fifties, but she didn't look a day over forty, and the smile she sent Nick now was full of mirth. "Did I wake you?"

Nick narrowed his eyes. He loved his mother, but she had an odd sense of humor. "You pinched my nose until I woke up. I think that was your intent."

"Of course it wasn't," Sharon soothed. "I'm just happy it worked out this way."

Nick rolled his eyes and stretched, taking a moment to let his mind clear. "How did you get in the house? I took your key away after you snuck in and had it cleaned last year and the maid threw all of my underwear away. Did you have a copy made?"

"I do have a copy, but that's not how I got in," Sharon said. "Did you know the glass pane in your back door is missing?"

"Yup."

"Do you want to tell me how that happened?"

"Probably not." Sharon waited. Nick tried to ignore her studied gaze, but finally he gave in. "Cassidy let herself into the house last night. I found her here when I got home."

"Oh, well, that's interesting," Sharon said, choosing her words carefully. "I was under the impression she was hiding from you. That was the talk of the town when I got my hair done the other day."

Nick stilled. His parents lived fifteen miles outside of Blackstone Bay, and while they still considered themselves part of the town, they weren't generally up on the day-to-day gossip. "You heard about that, huh?"

"You're one of the town highlights these days."

Nick pursed his lips.

"Cassidy is another," Sharon added.

"And, let me guess, Maddie is the third?"

"See, I shouldn't have to hear about these things from random people," Sharon said. "You should be calling me with nightly updates. I enjoy good town theater as much as the next person."

Nick made an exasperated sound in the back of his throat and rubbed his forehead ruefully. "I broke up with Cassidy last night."

"And a whole month late, too. I was way off in the pool."

Nick scowled. "You're my mother. You're supposed to be on my side."

"I am on your side," Sharon said. "That's why I think you should have broken up with Cassidy before Maddie returned to town."

"It's not like I knew she was coming home."

Sharon clucked sympathetically. "How did the breakup go?"

"Not well. She had kind of a meltdown."

"Worse than hiding for three days?"

"Yes."

"Well ... how is Maddie? I was actually surprised to find you here. I figured you would have been over there with her the second you were free."

Nick froze. "What do you mean?"

"Oh, don't do that, Nicholas Winters," Sharon chided. "I know very well that you and Maddie are officially on."

"No, we're not," Nick countered. Not yet, he internally conceded.

"I heard you and Maddie were on a date last night," Sharon pressed.

"We weren't on a date," Nick said. "I took her to the fair."

"And won her a stuffed animal."

"This town is like one big gossip mill," Nick grumbled. "I didn't win the stuffed animal. She won it for herself after I dropped twenty bucks trying to win it for her."

Sharon grinned. "She always was a stellar athlete. I heard she dunked you in the charity tank, too."

"Why are you even asking questions if you know all the answers?" Nick asked.

"I just wanted to see how you were doing," Sharon said, not chafing at her son's harsh tone. "I think your life has seen a lot of upheaval over the past few weeks. Maddie came home. You found out the truth about her. You saved her life. Now you're going to be a couple. That's a lot to deal with after ten years of pining."

Nick froze. "What did you just say?"

"I said that you're dealing with a lot."

"No, you said she told me the truth," Nick said, his voice icy. "What truth are you talking about?"

Sharon licked her lips as she met her son's angry gaze. "I know you know about Maddie being psychic. That's the only way you two could have gotten over everything and found a way to be together."

Nick was flabbergasted. "You knew?"

"Olivia and I were friends ... ."

Nick threw the covers off and climbed out of bed, being careful to give his mother a wide berth. "You knew!"

"I ... yes." Sharon's eyes clouded with concern. "Why are you so angry?"

"You knew why she left town," Nick challenged. "You knew why she left me. You knew how upset I was, and you didn't say a word. Why?"

"Because you weren't ready to deal with it, and Maddie wasn't ready to let you deal with it," Sharon replied, calm. "You two needed to find your way back together on your own. I knew it would happen eventually."

"She was alone," Nick argued. "We could have been together then."

"Do you think it would have lasted if you got together then?" Sharon asked.

"I ... ."

"Do you think you two were mature enough to take the ups and downs of Maddie's reality when you hadn't done any living yet?" Sharon pressed.

"Still ... ."

"Nick, I know you've always loved Maddie," Sharon said. "I know she's always loved you, too. Do you think Olivia wanted to let her go? It was hard on her. That was her only child. Maddie needed to find herself away from here, though. Olivia knew she would come back eventually. I think you knew, too. That's why you never let yourself get involved with someone seriously."

"What if I had gotten involved with someone seriously?" Nick challenged. "Would you have told me then?"

Sharon shrugged. "I don't know. I just knew that you didn't really want anyone but Maddie, so I let it ride. It didn't seem like you were hurting anyone. Everyone in town knew about your schedule. What happened with Cassidy was just ... unfortunate."

"I don't think she thinks it was just unfortunate," Nick said. "She's ... crushed."

"I think she's more jealous than anything else," Sharon said. "She wanted to be the one to break the cycle, and then she found that the reason for the cycle in the first place was Maddie, so she could never break the cycle. It was a vicious circle Cassidy could never get in front of."

"She's kind of gone off the deep end," Nick said, settling on the edge of his bed.

Sharon moved so she was sitting next to him. "Are you worried she's going to hurt you?"

"I don't think she's going to hurt me."

"Are you worried she's going to hurt Maddie?"

"If you had asked me that three weeks ago – or even three days ago – I would have said no," Nick said. "Now? I just ... you should have seen her. It was like looking at a stranger.

"The problem is, I never really got to know her in the first place," he continued. "I didn't care enough to get to know her. She kept trying to be exactly what she thought I wanted, but ... ."

"She could never be Maddie," Sharon finished. "You know how you treated Cassidy was wrong, right?"

"Yes."

"Did you apologize?"

"As many times as I could," Nick said, pinching the bridge of his nose. "I don't think it helped."

"You can't live your life according to Cassidy's feelings," Sharon said. "I think you've put your own happiness on hold for long enough. That's why I was surprised to find you here instead of with Maddie."

"Maddie hurt her ankle, and by the time I was done with Cassidy, it was late," Nick said. "I didn't want to wake her up. We need to have a long talk before anything happens."

"I thought the long talk would have occurred after you found out she was psychic."

"We had a long talk then, too," Nick said. "I just ... this is a different kind of talk."

"Right," Sharon said, smiling. "You just want to make sure you have all the ground rules in place."

"Exactly."

Sharon chuckled. "Honey, you're going to find that ground rules don't exist when you're dealing with love."

"It's going to be fine," Nick said. "I just ... I want to do this right."

"Then buy her some flowers," Sharon said.

"Flowers?"

"When a man goes courting, he should have flowers."

"I'm not going courting," Nick said. "Who even says that anymore?"

"This is going to be good," Sharon said, ignoring Nick's outburst. "You're finally going to get everything you want."

"You're for this? You want me with Maddie?"

"I've always wanted you with Maddie."

"Then how come you haven't been to see her since she got back into town?" Nick asked. "I assumed ... I assumed you were mad at her because you thought I was mad at her."

"First off, your issues are not my issues," Sharon said. "I love Maddie because I love her. Even if you hate her, I'll still love her. Second off, I thought Maddie needed some time to slip back into her life. I have every intention of seeing her. I just didn't want to put too much pressure on her. She's dealing with enough right now."

"What pressure are you going to put on her?"

Sharon got to her feet. "I finally have hope of a wedding, and grandchildren," she said.

"Mom! We're not even dating yet. Don't you dare say anything like that to her."

Sharon's smile was enigmatic as she moved toward the door. "Buy her red roses. That is the only flower that's acceptable when you start courting."

"You'd better stop using that word," Nick ordered.

"Have a good day, honey."

NICK WAS nervous when he walked into the flower shop and found Tara standing behind the counter. She was helping another customer, one Nick recognized right away.

"Mayor Higgins."

Sheldon Higgins had served as mayor of Blackstone Bay for almost ten years. He'd been a transport from Flint at the time, and since no one else wanted the job, he'd ran unopposed when the former mayor died. It wasn't even a full-time position, but Higgins seemed happy in his post. He was in his forties, and also worked as an accountant, but he seemed to thrive in the midst of small-town politics.

"Officer Winters," Higgins said, accepting the package of flowers from Tara. "How are you this fine festival day?"

Nick internally cringed. "I'm great. How are you?"

"I couldn't be better," Higgins said. "I love a good fair."

Nick was convinced the man had to be on uppers. He was never in a bad mood. "I do, too."

"Will you be returning today, or are you on duty?"

"I'm off today," Nick said. "We're technically all off. We just have to come in if we get a call. The sheriff just asked that we hang around the fair since that's where everyone will be."

"That's probably wise," Higgins said, shooting one more glance at Tara. "Thank you, my dear. I can't tell you how nice it is to have you in our town. You're just ... radiant."

"I guess that's why you come to visit me every week to buy flowers," she said.

"Maybe I just like seeing you," Higgins teased.

Tara's smile was even, and she didn't let it slip until Higgins left the store. Once he was gone, Tara turned to Nick. "Do you ever think he's weird?"

"Define weird."

"He's an outsider, and I know that since I'm an outsider, I shouldn't be suspicious of other outsiders, but he's just so ... ."

"Happy?" Nick interjected.

"Yeah. I don't trust anyone who is always happy."

Nick didn't say it out loud, but he couldn't help but agree.

"He's also young," Tara said. "He's forty, and yet he spends all of his free time going to events at the senior center."

"Maybe he just likes old ladies," Nick suggested. "They fawn all over him. It's probably good for his ego."

"And he doesn't date, right?"

Nick furrowed his brow. "I guess not. Huh. I'd never thought about that. You're right. That is weird."

"He's a good-looking guy," Tara said. "So, why doesn't he date?"

"Maybe he's gay," Nick said. "He might not want to out himself in a town as small as Blackstone Bay."

"Well, if that's the case, I feel sorry for him," Tara said. "He shouldn't have to hide who he is."

"What else would it be?" Nick asked.

"I don't know," Tara said, shrugging. "There's just something off about him. I can't put my finger on it. So, what can I get for you?"

Nick realized he was in an awkward position. "I need some flowers."

"Okay. What do you want?"

"I ... um ... ."

Tara took pity on him. "Are you trying to say 'I'm sorry' to one girl or 'I love you' to the other?"

Nick pursed his lips. "I need a dozen red roses."

"Ah, love it is." Tara turned to the refrigerated case behind her and gathered the blooms. When she returned to the counter to arrange the flowers in a box, she regarded Nick seriously. "Have you gotten a chance to talk to Cassidy?"

"I talked to her last night," Nick said. "I'm actually surprised she didn't call you."

"How did she take it?"

Nick wasn't sure how to proceed. Talking out of turn seemed like a bad way to go, but Cassidy obviously needed a friend. "Not well."

"Well, at least it's over with," Tara said pragmatically, snipping a few of the rose stems shorter and fitting plastic water basins on the ends. "She needed to know. I know she was fighting dealing with it, but it will be better now."

"I think she's going to be worse for a little while," Nick admitted. "She seems ... bitter."

"I know," Tara said. "I'll look for her when I'd done here. Maybe a night with a bottle of wine and a whole lot of complaining will help her get it out of her system."

"Maybe," Nick said. "I just ... I'm sorry. If it helps, I really am sorry."

"I think everyone knows you're sorry," Tara said. "I think even Cassidy knows you're sorry. She's feeling too sorry for herself to look at the big picture right now, though. I think she's always known you weren't the one for her. She wanted it to be different, but you can't force a situation like that."

"Thanks," Nick said. "You don't have to be nice to me, though. I know it's your duty to hate me. It's okay. I've earned it."

"Something tells me you'll be fine," Tara said, handing the flower box to Nick and punching a few numbers into the register. "I think a certain blonde is going to love her flowers, by the way."

"I hope so," Nick said, handing over his credit card. "We have a lot of things to talk about."

Tara snorted. "Yeah. Most men drop a hundred bucks on flowers because they have talking on their mind."

Nick blushed furiously. "I ... ."

"Oh, you're so cute," Tara teased. "I think this is the first time I've seen you stumble."

"I'm not stumbling."

"No, you're not," Tara agreed. "You're just starting the race."

17. SEVENTEEN

"I am not doing this again," Maddie said, leaning back in her chair and extending her sore ankle out in front of her. "Three days of reading tarot cards has completely sapped my energy. I feel like I'm eighty – and crippled."

Christy smirked. "How much money have you made, though?"

"A lot," Maddie conceded. "The money is going to keep me flush for months. I know I shouldn't complain, but I'm just exhausted."

The two women had closed the psychic tent down for the afternoon and were now reclining in front of fans as they regrouped. Maddie hadn't seen Nick all day, and she was worried. She was worried he hadn't found Cassidy the night before, and she was even more worried he had and she'd somehow changed his mind.

The truth was, Maddie was a bigger ball of nerves now than she had been before she admitted being psychic to Nick.

Christy studied her friend with a bemused look on her face. "You still haven't heard from Nick, have you?"

"I'm not Nick's keeper," Maddie sniffed.

"Oh, good grief," Christy said, laughing. "You're just all ... fluttery."

"I am not fluttery."

"Oh, but you are," Christy said. "You need to focus on something else. I'm sure Nick will be by to make a grand proclamation of love any second now. Until then, let's talk about something else."

"Great," Maddie said. "What do you want to talk about?"

"When you were skinny-dipping with Nick the other night, did you get to see anything good?"

Maddie frowned.

Christy held up her hand. "I was just joking. How is Maude?"

"She's on some quest to keep Harriet Proctor from becoming a Pink Lady," Maddie said. "Now that you mention it, though, I didn't see Granny last night. I hope she's not in jail."

Christy chortled. "Nick would tell you if she was. I'm actually surprised Harriet wants to be a Pink Lady. All of the women in that group hate her. She should just start her own group."

"You should suggest it to her."

"I just might," Christy said. "She has an appointment this week. She gets her hair set once a week. I don't think she washes it in between visits. It's always greasy and gross when she comes in."

"That's ... nice."

"I like the idea of rival gangs of old women in town," Christy mused. "It will be like the Bloods and the Crips, but instead we'll have the Liver Spots and the Replacement Hips."

Maddie couldn't stop herself from laughing.

"Think about it," Christy continued. "They'll have blood feuds on every corner. There will be Geritol flying from speeding cars. There will be Metamucil dropping into meeting rooms like napalm. There will be dentures left like horse heads in rivals' beds."

"Cute," Maddie said. "Very cute."

"What else is going on?" Christy asked, sobering. "Tell me about the guy who went after Tara."

"There's not much to tell," Maddie said. "I can't describe him, other to say he's about six-feet tall and thin. The hoodie made it impossible to see if he was muscular or just fit. I couldn't see his face. His hands were white, but since there aren't any black people in Blackstone Bay, that shouldn't come as too much of a surprise."

"We do really need to get some color here," Christy mused. "Even the owner of the Middle Eastern restaurant is white."

Maddie snorted. "The food is still good, though."

"The food is excellent," Christy agreed. "What do you think the guy wanted? Do you think he wanted to hurt her? Do you think he found you by accident last night? Do you think you're his new target?"

Maddie froze. She hadn't considered that. "I don't know," she said finally. "Everything just happened so fast. I didn't know what to think. It does seem a little too coincidental that he would just happen upon me there, doesn't it?"

"What does Nick think?"

"Nick had other things on his mind."

"Like going after Cassidy?"

Maddie nodded.

"I'm sure he'll be by soon," Christy said. "It was probably just an emotional night. Cassidy probably cried a lot."

"No, Cassidy did not cry."

Maddie and Christy shifted in their seats as Cassidy burst through the flaps.

"Cassidy," Christy said, her tone dry. "How are you this hot and humid day?"

Maddie wanted to kick her, but her ankle was too sore to try. "Cassidy, how are you?"

"Can you give us a few minutes alone?" Cassidy asked Christy pointedly. "We have a few things to discuss."

"No," Christy said. "Maddie is already injured, and you left her in a vulnerable position last night. I'm not going to make the same mistake."

"Excuse me? What are you talking about?" Cassidy's face was flushed, a mixture of anger and confusion warring for supremacy.

"Maddie was attacked right after you left her last night," Christy charged. "Was that a coincidence, or did you hire someone to try and take her out?"

"Christy!" Maddie shook her head firmly. "No one is blaming you for what happened last night," she said, turning back to Cassidy. "I wasn't hurt."

"You reinjured your ankle," Christy pointed out.

"I ... that wasn't Cassidy's fault," Maddie said. "That was my fault. I tripped."

"I don't even understand what you're saying," Cassidy snapped. "I'm here to talk about what you did to me last night. Not everything is about you."

Maddie stilled. "What did I do to you last night?"

"You know exactly what you did."

"Oh, Nick finally found you and dropped the hammer," Christy said, nodding her head sympathetically. "I'm sorry."

"You're not sorry," Cassidy charged. "Your friend got exactly what she wanted, so you're happy. My feelings don't matter to you. Don't pretend that they do."

"I'm sorry for you," Christy said. "I genuinely am. Maddie didn't do anything to you, though."

"She's the one who has been whispering in Nick's ear. She's the one who told him to dump me. She's the one who is playing with him to get what she wants."

"You don't even know Maddie," Christy said. "You shouldn't accuse her of things she hasn't done."

"Oh, I know Maddie," Cassidy said. "I've known girls like her my whole life. She's the kind of girl who only wants something when someone else has it. She didn't want Nick when she left, but she came back and found him happy with someone else, and then she wanted him."

"That's not what happened," Maddie said, biting her bottom lip.

"It is what happened," Cassidy said. "I know. Don't tell me what I do and don't know."

Christy held up her hands in mock surrender. "Listen, I think you're ... overwrought. Did you get any sleep last night? Have you gotten any sleep over the past few days? You know that sleep deprivation can mess you up more than alcohol, right?"

Cassidy made a face. "Are you accusing me of being crazy?"

"Crazy is a harsh word," Christy said.

"That's what you're saying, though."

"It is," Christy agreed. "You're acting like a crazy person."

"I am not crazy," Cassidy seethed. "I know exactly what happened to me. I know that your friend purposely ruined my life. She's a ... whore."

Maddie reared back as if she'd been slapped, tears filling her eyes. "I'm sorry. I ... ."

"Don't apologize to her," Christy snapped. "She's upset. This isn't your fault, though."

"Oh, that's right, Maddie can't fight her own battles," Cassidy said. "She doesn't need to. Everyone in town does it for her."

Maddie struggled to her feet, her cheeks hot as she fought the urge to cry. "I really am sorry."

"I don't believe you," Cassidy said. "You've gotten everything you've ever wanted. You're not sorry for anything. You're an evil woman. You're a user. You're an evil user. You don't care who you hurt as long as you get your own way. I wish you'd never returned to Blackstone Bay."

Maddie moved toward the front of the tent, the need to escape overwhelming her. "I'm sorry," she mumbled again.

"In fact, I wish you'd just die!" Cassidy exploded.

NICK PICKED that moment to enter the tent, his box of flowers gripped tightly to his chest. He was nervous ... but ready. That's why Maddie pushing past him and fleeing into the fair crowd before he could even utter a word took him by surprise.

"Maddie?" He glanced between Christy and Cassidy, curious. "What's going on?"

Cassidy had the grace to look abashed. "It was nothing. She's just sensitive."

"Cassidy just called Maddie a whore and wished she was dead," Christy replied, nonplussed.

"That is not what I said," Cassidy shot back.

"That is exactly what you said," Christy said. "I left out the part where you called her evil."

Nick rubbed the palm of his hand against his forehead, flustered. "I thought we talked all of this out last night. I thought … ."

"What? You thought what?" Cassidy asked, her hands on her hips. "You thought you could buy me those flowers and smooth everything over?"

Nick looked at the flowers, confused. "No."

"Well, it's not going to work," Cassidy said. "I told you that I wasn't going to take you back when Maddie hurt you. I don't care how many boxes of flowers you buy for me." She held her hands out. "I still want the flowers, though."

Nick sent a mental plea for help in Christy's direction. Cassidy was clearly losing it.

"I don't think those flowers are for you," Christy said, tipping Nick's arm down so she could get a better look. "A dozen red roses. Nice."

"But … ." Cassidy's eyes were busy as they darted around the tent. "Why are you here? Didn't you come because you knew I'd be here?"

"No," Nick replied honestly. "I came to see Maddie." He saw no reason to lie. Cassidy was still living in a fantasy world where Nick was going to come crawling back to her. He had to shatter her extremely unrealistic delusion.

Cassidy either didn't understand what was going on or she was refusing to acknowledge it. Nick wasn't sure which one was more likely, but he was having a hard time believing she could be that oblivious.

"The flowers are for Maddie," Christy said, her tone even. "He was coming to … ." Christy held her hands up, helpless. "He was bringing her the flowers. He was coming to see her. Seriously. I think you're sleep deprived. You should go home and get some rest."

Realization dawned on Cassidy. Finally. "You were coming here to profess your love for her."

Nick remained calm. "Cassidy, I told you all of this last night. I told you I was sorry. I told you I would forever feel guilty for how I treated you. I also told you that I want to be with Maddie."

"But .... ."

"No," Nick said, shaking his head. "No buts. Nothing has changed. Nothing is going to change. You just need to accept it."

Cassidy looked like she was about to burst into tears. Instead, her hand snaked out and she slapped Nick as hard as she could across the face. The sound of her palm making contact with his solid jaw echoed throughout the tent, and Nick rocked backward due to the force.

"I hope you both die," Cassidy said, her eyes dark and narrow. "I hope you both are unhappy and die."

Nick watched her storm out of the tent, stunned. "I don't even know what to say."

"I've never seen her like that," Christy said, getting to her feet. "I ... she needs sleep. That's all I can think. She probably hasn't slept more than a few hours over the past few days. If she gets some sleep, she'll probably be ashamed of what she's done."

"I hope you're right," Nick said, sighing wearily. "I hope you're right."

"The good news is, I won the pool," Christy said. "I see some shoe shopping in my future. I believe you have a blonde to chase down, too."

Nick nodded.

"The good news is, she's hobbled," Christy said. "You should be able to catch up with her pretty quickly."

"I'm on it," Nick said. "Hey, Christy?"

Christy glanced back at him, an eyebrow arched.

"Thank you for being such a good friend to Maddie."

Christy smiled. "Go and get your girl. You can thank me with lilies tomorrow."

MADDIE MANAGED to limp the four blocks home, although the tears she was trying to fight off overcame her before she could escape to her inner sanctum. She knew she was being ridiculous. She couldn't help but feel guilty for what she'd done, though.

Had she really ruined Cassidy's life? Even if it wasn't true, perception was a funny thing, and Cassidy's perception was telling her that Maddie was to blame for all of the unhappiness in her life.

When Maddie made it to the front steps of the house, she stilled long enough to study the box of flowers on the front stoop. *Where had these come from?* Nick had been holding flowers. She'd only gotten a brief glimpse of him before fleeing, but she'd seen the flowers resting in his arms. Had he bought two boxes?

Maddie struggled to lean over, and when she opened the box she took an involuntarily step back. The flowers inside weren't vibrant blooms reflecting love, but decayed remnants of flowers long since dead. There was a note inside, and Maddie reached for it despite the warning alarm dinging in the recesses of her mind. Her hands were shaking when she opened it. There was only one word on the card: Soon.

18. EIGHTEEN

Maddie's back was to him when Nick approached her on the porch. She was staring at something by her feet, but he couldn't see what. He hopped up the stairs, and Maddie practically flew out of her skin when she heard the noise, jumping away from him when he reached for her.

"Maddie? What's wrong?"

Maddie pointed to the flowers on the ground. Nick shifted his own box of flowers into her hands and knelt down. "These don't look … ." He didn't know what to say.

Maddie handed him the card, mute.

Nick glanced at it briefly. "Get inside."

He left the dead flowers on the porch and pressed his body against Maddie's as he pushed her through the front door. Once they were on the other side, he swept her up in his arms and carried her over to the window seat.

"Sit here, love. I'll be back in a minute."

Nick was all business, and since Maddie was an emotional mess, she was taking his clipped tone to heart. "Okay."

Nick sighed, recognizing the wary tone of her voice. He kissed her forehead quickly and cupped the back of her head as he forced her gaze to lock onto his. "It's going to be okay. I just have to make a call. You're safe here."

"I ... ."

"We're going to have a long talk in a little bit, Mad," he said. "We can't get into it now. I have to call Kreskin, and I don't want to start now and get interrupted. Do you want something to drink?"

Maddie shook her head.

"I'll get you some iced tea after I call Kreskin," Nick said. "Just ... stay right there for me, okay? Don't you dare move."

"WHAT DO YOU THINK?" Kreskin asked, studying the box of dead flowers as Nick sealed the card into a plastic bag.

"I think whoever was focused on Tara the other night is now focused on Maddie." Nick and Kreskin were outside, the door to the house closed to cut them off from prying ears. "I think Maddie is in danger."

"Are you sure this isn't just some sick joke?" Kreskin asked.

"Who would do that?"

Kreskin pinched the bridge of his nose. "What about Cassidy?"

Nick stilled. "You don't think ... ?"

"I've heard a few things over the past few days," Kreskin said. "I heard she was hiding from you because she knew you were going to break up with her. I also heard she had some sort of ... kerfuffle ... with Maddie last night. The witnesses said that right after Cassidy left Maddie claimed a man in a hoodie approached her."

"You don't think it's a coincidence," Nick mused. "You think that either Cassidy left these flowers or whoever the guy in the hoodie is left them because he's working with Cassidy."

"Are you denying it's a possibility?"

"I don't know," Nick replied honestly. "Cassidy is unhinged. She just attacked Maddie down at the fair."

"Physically?"

"No. She just wished Maddie was dead. She then wished I was dead, too."

"You've officially broken up with her, right?" Kreskin asked, glancing in through the window where Maddie was sitting with another box of flowers cradled against her chest. "Those aren't dead flowers, too, are they?"

"Those are from me," Nick said.

"I guess that answers the breakup question," Kreskin said. "How did she take it?"

"Not well. She broke into my house last night. She had specific ... intentions ... which I shot down. I then handled the breakup situation to the best of my ability."

"It didn't go over well, did it?"

"Nope."

"Okay, let's think about it for a minute," Kreskin said, straightening. "If Cassidy left the flowers, it's probably just some woman thing. If Cassidy hired the guy in the hoodie, that's a whole other issue. She could be really dangerous."

"I'm worried about Maddie," Nick said.

"Well, then I guess it's good she's got a police officer to take care of her," Kreskin teased. "Look at it this way, you have a viable reason to stay here tonight. You don't even have to wait until the third date to make your move."

Nick scowled. "I don't need an excuse to spend the night here. I've spent the night here several times since she's been back in town, I'll have you know."

"Yeah, but before you had Cassidy as a barrier," Kreskin said. "Now you're going to have no choice but to show her how manly you are."

Nick punched Kreskin's shoulder lightly. "Let it go."

Kreskin grinned. "I don't blame you for being nervous," he said. "Maddie almost died a few weeks ago. You almost died when you tried to save her. I get it. Just ... this could be nothing but a bitter woman getting a little revenge."

"I'd like to believe that," Nick replied. "That still doesn't explain why the guy in the hoodie went after Tara first."

Kreskin pursed his lips, considering. "Maybe he was told to go after someone else first, so the suspicion wouldn't land on Cassidy if it was just Maddie."

"Except Tara is Cassidy's friend."

"I don't know," Kreskin said. "I'll have the flowers and note sent to the state crime lab. Until then ... just keep the blonde close."

"Don't worry about that," Nick said, his eyes meeting Maddie's through the glass. "I won't let her out of my sight."

"I'm sure you won't," Kreskin said, his tone teasing and light. "Just try to pace yourself."

"WHAT DID HE SAY?" Maddie asked, sipping her iced tea as Nick approached the window seat.

Nick lifted her feet carefully, paying special attention to her injured ankle, and shifted her farther into the window seat so he could settle beside her. "He's worried that Cassidy left them for you."

"Do you think she did?"

"I don't know," Nick said. "She's completely lost it. Even if Cassidy left the flowers, that doesn't explain the guy in the hoodie who went after Tara, or why he went after you last night. Kreskin thinks it's a possibility that Cassidy hired him, or that he's working with her for another reason, but I'm not sure that makes sense."

"Where did you find Cassidy last night?"

"She broke into my house."

Maddie shifted, her eyes widening. "Are you kidding?"

"No." Nick gripped Maddie's hand and brought it to his lips. "We had a long talk and I told her that it was over. She didn't take it well, but she knows."

"I figured that much out when she came to the tent," Maddie said. "She was angry."

"Christy told me what she said to you," Nick said. "I need you not to take any of that stuff to heart. It's not your fault. You didn't hurt her. That's on me."

"She wants me dead. She said it."

"I'm hoping that's just grief talking," Nick said. "Or temporary insanity."

"What if it's not?"

"I won't let her hurt you, Mad. I won't let anyone hurt you."

Maddie rested her head against Nick's shoulder. He smiled down at her. "Why haven't you opened your flowers?"

"I didn't know they were for me," Maddie said.

"Who else did you think they were for?"

"I ... ."

"Open them, Mad."

Maddie concentrated on the box as she opened it, smiling at the twelve perfect blooms. "They're beautiful."

"You're beautiful."

Maddie worried her bottom lip with her teeth. "Thank you."

"Okay, Mad, it's time for us to talk," Nick said. "You need to get comfortable." He gathered the flower box and her iced tea glass and moved them over to the tarot table.

"I should probably put those in water," Maddie said.

Nick knew she was stalling for time. "They have those little green things with water on each stem. They'll be fine for a little while. I'm not letting you get out of this conversation. I've gone through hell the past few days so we can have it, and we're going to have it now."

Nick climbed back up into the window seat, shifting a bevy of times before he could get comfortable. He felt itchy. He knew it wasn't the stacked pillows fighting against him, though. It was destiny. "I want to be with you, Maddie."

Maddie's eyes filled with hope. "You do?"

"You can't possibly be surprised. I've made my intentions pretty obvious for weeks now."

"I just ... I wasn't sure," Maddie said. "This afternoon, when I hadn't seen you, I kind of convinced myself that you'd decided to stay with Cassidy."

Nick barked out a hoarse laugh. "You don't ever have to worry about me wanting to be with someone else," he said. "I've never wanted to be with anyone else."

"Never?"

"Never. I've only ever wanted you." Nick's eyes were serious as they bore into Maddie's sea-blue orbs. "The question is, do you want to be with me?"

Maddie inhaled deeply. "I've always loved you, Nicky. I never thought you could possibly love me the same way I loved you. You were the handsome and popular jock, and I was the mousy and … ."

"Mad, don't," Nick said. "If you start talking badly about yourself, I'm going to have to beat you up."

"Let me get this out, Nicky," Maddie pleaded. "I know you never treated me like I was less than anyone else, but I always felt it. I really wish I'd told you the truth back then because I might not have hurt you – and myself – if I could have just had faith."

Nick felt tears prickling the backs of his eyes. "My mom came to see me today," he said, cutting her off before she could go any further. "She knows, by the way. Olivia told her. She's known for a long time."

Maddie's eyes widened. "Oh."

"I was mad at first," Nick said. "I was mad because she didn't tell me. If she had, I would have gone after you. I would have moved south to be with you. We could have been together then. We wouldn't have lost ten years together. Do you know what she said?"

Maddie shook her head, her blonde hair brushing against her shoulders.

"She said I wasn't ready to know the truth and you weren't ready for me to know the truth," Nick said. "She said that we weren't equipped to be together then. I was still mad, but I think she might have been right. If we'd tried to be together then, we probably wouldn't have made it. We were too young.

"So, the thing is, Mad, I'm not angry you didn't tell me now," he continued. "I think you ended up saving us. I'm not going to pretend it didn't hurt, but I don't want to think about it for one more day. We can't go back in time. We have a chance here. Well, we have a chance if you want us to have one."

Maddie pressed her lips together, a lone tear cascading down her cheek.

"Don't cry, Mad," Nick said, reaching over to catch the tear. "If you don't want to be with me, we'll figure something out. You're still my best friend."

"That's what I'm afraid of," Maddie said.

Nick stilled. "What?"

"What if you decide that you don't really want me? What if you just think you do? I know I'm always going to love you, but if we do this, and you realize that I'm not what you want, we'll lose everything."

"We're not going to lose anything, Maddie," Nick said. "I've never loved anyone but you. I'll never want anyone but you. This is our chance to get everything we've ever wanted. I'm not going to get tired of you, and I'm not going to want anyone else because I suddenly get bored. Where you're concerned, I'll never get bored."

"What if ... ?" Maddie wasn't sure if she could continue, so she snapped her mouth shut. Nick sighed and waited. "I haven't had a lot of experience with ... ."

Nick was confused. When he realized what she was getting at, he sat up straighter. "Are you saying you're still a ... virgin?"

"No," Maddie replied, shaking her head. "I've had sex a few times. I just know you've had a lot of ... practice. What if I'm bad? What if I don't turn you on? What if ... ?"

Nick grabbed her chin and forced her gaze to him. "Stop that right now," he ordered. "I don't care how much practice you've had. We're not even going to deal with that right away anyway."

Maddie blanched. "What?"

"I'm putting a moratorium on the sex talk," Nick said. "We need some time together as a couple first. So, I hereby declare that we're not having sex for at least two weeks."

"Two weeks?"

"We'll talk about it again then," Nick said. "I want you to feel comfortable with me first."

"I always feel comfortable with you, Nicky."

"Yeah?" Nick rubbed his thumb over her chin. "I haven't done this before, though."

Nick slammed his mouth against Maddie's, sucking in a huge gulp of air to steady himself as he went. Her lips felt like soft pillows against his, and when their mouths met, it was like coming home after a long trip. She was so surprised, she gasped at his actions. Nick remained still for a moment, almost crying out in relief when she wrapped her hands around the back of his head and held him close.

Nick slid his hands over her jaw gently and rested them against her neck before tangling them in her hair and pulling her on top of him. His mouth never left hers, and she was making soft sighing noises into his mouth as he kissed her.

Ten years of need were driving them both, and Nick had no intention of letting her go now. He was surprised when her lips parted and her tongue darted out to touch his. He tightened his hands in her hair as she shifted so she was completely on top of him.

Their lips were fused now, and they didn't pull away for what felt like forever. When they finally parted, they were both gasping. Chest to chest, both could feel the hammering of the other's heart as they beat against each other.

"Wow," Maddie breathed, her eyes sparkling.

"Wow," Nick agreed. He brushed her hair away from her forehead. "I need to do that again."

This time, when their lips met, the kiss was softer and less needy, but still full of desire. It was going to be okay, Nick realized. Everything was going to be okay. They were finally on the same page in their story, and the book was going to have a happy ending. He wouldn't let anything come between them again.

19. NINETEEN

"Have you eaten?"

Maddie's head was resting on Nick's chest, and they'd been quiet for about a half hour when he decided to stir. When she shifted her head, his fingers rolling through her flaxen tresses, he noticed her lips were slightly swollen from hours of kissing. She looked so beautiful he just wanted to kiss her again.

"I had breakfast this morning," Maddie murmured.

"It's after six, love," Nick said. "You need food."

"I don't want to move," she admitted.

"I'm not particularly fond of the idea either," he said. "However, I'm starving. We also need to get your flowers into a vase. We're not sleeping down here tonight either."

Maddie shifted, her eyes widening slightly.

"We still have a two-week moratorium, Mad, so don't get all worked up," Nick said. "We're just not sleeping down here where Maude could walk in and ... do something Maude-like."

Maddie giggled. God, he loved that sound. "Come on." Nick shifted Maddie so he could pick her up and then climbed out of the window seat. "Do you have anything to eat in this house?"

"I don't know," Maddie admitted. "Speaking of Granny, don't you think we should've seen her?"

"Kreskin said he saw her down at the fair this afternoon," Nick said. "I was worried about the flowers showing up and her not being here. Apparently, she and Irma were wearing big, floppy hats and following Harriet around."

"They didn't have guns, did they?"

Nick snickered. "No. I'm hoping she'll be busy enough to stay away for a while, though. It would be nice to spend a couple hours in complete solitude with you."

"Isn't that what we've been doing?"

Nick set Maddie down in a chair by the table and grinned. "A couple more then. Do you want me to try to find something to eat here, or just order pizza?"

"Pizza."

"No onions," Nick teased.

"No onions."

Nick pulled his cell phone out of his pocket and placed the order. When he was done, he excused himself to wash his face, and when he returned to the kitchen he found Maddie standing behind the counter and organizing her roses in a vase.

"You shouldn't be on your ankle," Nick chided, walking up behind her and wrapping his arms around her waist.

"You can't carry me around everywhere."

"I work out."

"I noticed."

Nick kissed her cheek, inhaling her scent happily. "I can arrange those for you if you want to sit down."

"Nope. They're mine. I want to do it. I've never gotten flowers from someone before."

Nick's heart stuttered. "Well, you'll be getting a lot from me."

"That's not really necessary," Maddie said. "I just ... want you. I don't need flowers."

Nick tightened his arms and held her close. "You'll always have me. You're going to get flowers, too. I even have to buy Christy lilies for being such a good friend to you."

"You should buy her the whole flower shop."

"That might be cheaper over the long run."

After dinner and dishes, Nick insisted on carrying Maddie up the narrow staircase that led to the second floor of the old Victorian. He settled her on the bed and then glanced around, suddenly nervous. "This is weird."

"It's not like you haven't been in here before," Maddie said.

"I know. This is just different." He shook his head to ward off the unease and then moved to her dresser. "What do you want to sleep in?"

Maddie arched an eyebrow. "Um, I don't know. I usually just sleep in a tank top and cotton shorts."

Nick pulled a pair of plaid boxers out of the drawer. They were tiny enough to make his head spin. "These?"

"Those are fine."

Nick tossed the shorts and a tank top in her direction. "Change your clothes. I'm going to make sure everything is locked up downstairs. I'll be back in a few minutes."

Maddie looked relieved. "Okay."

"I'll be right back."

After checking every window and door in the house (twice), Nick returned to Maddie's bedroom and found her sitting on the edge of her bed braiding her hair.

"What are you doing?" he asked softly.

"My hair will be a mess in the morning if I don't braid it."

"I like it loose."

Maddie glanced over her shoulder. "I'll look like Medusa."

"I don't care," Nick said. "I want to be able to feel your hair all night. I love your hair."

Maddie blew out a sigh and slowly unbraided what she'd started. "Fine. If you make one joke tomorrow, though, I'll never leave it loose again."

"Deal." Nick stripped off his shirt, not missing the way Maddie's eyes scanned his chest before shifting quickly. It was going to be a long two weeks, but he wasn't backing down on his moratorium. He wanted them to have some time together before they took the next step. He wanted to remember every moment of their journey, and he wanted time to savor every new experience. He was perfectly happy kissing her for the time being.

After dropping his jeans, Nick hit the light switch and crawled into Maddie's bed with her, loving the way the cool sheets felt as they drifted down on top of him. He could feel Maddie's body as she instinctively shifted closer to him.

"You know you can touch me now, right?" Nick teased.

Maddie placed her hand over his heart, and Nick slipped his arm under her body and drew her close so she could rest her head against his chest. "You're sure you don't want to ... ?"

"Not yet, Mad," Nick said. "When it happens, it's going to be special, and we're not going to have anything hanging over our heads. All I want to do is hold you tonight. Two weeks. I told you."

"I feel like I've been sentenced," Maddie said, giggling.

"You have," Nick said, kissing her forehead. "You've been sentenced to life."

Maddie sighed as she shifted her chin so she could kiss him. Nick met her searching lips with a happy moan. After a few minutes of wandering hands and fervent tongues, Maddie snuggled into his warmth. "I love you, Nicky."

Nick choked up. "I love you, Mad. I love you so much."

"WELL, well, well. Look what we have here."

Maddie lifted her head, her mind still muddled with sleep and focused on her grandmother. Maude was standing next to the bed, hands on hips, and she was staring down at Maddie with a knowing look.

It took Maddie a minute to realize where she was, and who was holding her in his arms as he wiped the sleep from his eyes.

"Don't you knock, Maude?"

"Not in my own house," she replied. "What are you two doing?"

"Sleeping," Nick said. "Well, we were until you showed up. Where were you all night, by the way?"

"That's none of your business," Maude chided. "You two need to get up and get dressed. We all have to have a pow-wow in the kitchen."

Maddie was surprised. She thought her grandmother would be excited about the new development. "But ... ."

"Now," Maude said, turning on her heel and stalking out of the room.

Once she was gone, Maddie fixed her contemplative eyes on Nick. "Do you think she's mad?"

"Mad angry or mad crazy?"

Maddie shrugged.

"She's definitely crazy," Nick said. "I have no idea if she's angry, and I don't care." He pressed his lips to Maddie's mouth and greeted her properly. "Good morning, love."

"Good morning," Maddie murmured.

Nick looked her hair over. It was bigger than usual but entirely adorable. "You don't look like Medusa."

"That's probably because I slept like a rock," she said. "I didn't even dream. I always dream."

"You didn't need to dream," Nick teased. "Your dream was already in bed with you."

"Oh, you have such a big ego."

"I do," Nick agreed, throwing the covers off the two of them. "Put a robe on. I managed to keep my hands from slipping in the dark because I couldn't see you in those tiny shorts. There's no way I can do it now."

"Even in front of Granny?"

"You have no idea what those stupid little shorts are doing to me," Nick said. "I'm going to the bathroom. Put a robe on. I'm not kidding. If you don't, I'm going to forget my moratorium and Maude is going to walk in on something else."

Maddie's cheeks colored.

Nick kissed her one more time for good measure. "I love you."

Maddie's relaxed. "I love you."

"Get dressed," he said. "If we're lucky, Maude will make us breakfast while she lectures us. I still love her waffles."

"I hope she doesn't yell at me."

"Don't worry. I'm pretty sure I can take her."

"WE HAVE A VERY SERIOUS SITUATION," Maude said, sliding a plate of waffles in front of Nick. "We're going to have to approach it like adults, and come to a resolution."

Maddie squared her shoulders. "Okay. Why don't you tell me your main concern."

Maude nodded. "Harriet Proctor has managed to buy two votes on the Pink Lady Council. Now, I was out all night trying to sway Gertie and Bella to see the light, but whatever Harriet did to bribe them was significant. So, Nick, I need you to arrest Gertie and Bella. I don't care if you have to trump up charges. They can't sit on the council if they have charges pending. That's going to be enough to buy me some time."

Maddie stilled while Nick speared a large hunk of waffles with his fork and doused them with syrup. "I'm not arresting Gertie and Bella."

"You have to," Maude said. "I can't figure out another solution. Harriet may actually have enough votes to get herself invited into the club. If that happens, then I'm going to go to jail because I'll murder her."

"You're just going to suck it up," Nick said. He tapped Maddie's plate. "Eat. You need food."

Maddie was confused. "Wait, that's what you wanted to talk about? You want Nick to arrest Gertie and Bella?"

"Of course," Maude said. "He's a big, old disappointment, though. First, he couldn't win the pool for me, and now this. You're out of my will, boy."

Nick raised an eyebrow, blasé. "I'm sorry I've crushed you so horribly. Please forgive me."

"I thought ... ." Maddie glanced at Nick for support. "I thought you were mad about finding us up in my bed."

"Why would I be mad about that?" Maude asked. "It's your house. Although, for future reference, you should probably lock the door."

"Oh, don't worry," Nick said, nonplussed. "I'm replacing that doorknob today."

"I thought you were mad because ... ."

"You had sex?" Maude asked. "I've been waiting for you two to have sex for weeks. It was only a matter of time. Once I lost in the pool, I didn't care when it happened."

"We didn't have sex," Maddie said, scandalized.

Maude looked at Nick for confirmation.

"I put a moratorium on sex for two weeks," he explained. "I didn't want her to fixate on it too much when we were just starting out. It seemed like the easiest course of action. Can I have more waffles?"

Maude grabbed another plate from the counter and slid it in front of him. "If you didn't have sex, why are you so hungry?"

"Because we made out for hours after some very emotional admissions," he replied, guileless. "And before that, I had a long night breaking up with Cassidy."

"Yeah, I heard about that," Maude said. "Did she really break into your house?"

"Who told you?"

"Your mother has a big mouth," Maude replied. "It's really unforgivable."

Nick rolled his eyes. "She's unbelievable. While you're here, though, I need to have a serious discussion with you, too."

"Oh, is this about the guy in the hoodie who went after Maddie the other night? Or is this about the dead flowers and threatening note on the porch yesterday?"

"Kreskin apparently has a big mouth, too," Nick grumbled. "Yes. I need you to be careful. Someone has zeroed in on Maddie."

"It's probably just Cassidy," Maude said.

"Cassidy is not masquerading as a six-foot-tall man in a hoodie," Nick said. "I'm not denying the flowers might be from her, but the man is a real danger. That means you have to be careful. I don't care if you want to run all over the town with Irma or Catherine or whoever else is plotting doom and destruction against Harriet. You can't wander around alone, though."

"Fine."

"I'm not joking," Nick said.

"I said fine," Maude replied, irritated.

Nick studied her for one more moment and then turned back to his breakfast. "Eat, Maddie. You're going to need your strength today."

"Why? What are we doing?"

Nick grinned. "We're going swimming down at the lake. We're taking a picnic and making a day out of it."

"We are?"

"Oh, yeah," Nick said. "I've been dying to get you back in the water when it's light out and I can actually see something."

Maddie was blushing furiously. "Nicky."

"Oh, grow up, Maddie," Maude said. "You finally have everything you've ever wanted. Why don't you just relax and enjoy it?"

"I agree," Nick said. "Bathing suits are optional today."

Maude cuffed him on the back of the head. "Don't get fresh."

"You just said … ."

"I didn't say you could do it in front of me," Maude protested. "I'm her grandmother."

"Fine," Nick said, rubbing his head. "You're kind of mean today."

Maude smiled. "And you two are kind of happy. It's about time."

"It is," Nick agreed, smiling at Maddie. "It definitely is."

20. TWENTY

"Faster."

Nick arched an eyebrow. "Excuse me?"

"You have to move faster," Maddie said, refusing to back down. "You're never going to catch that turtle if you're going to be that slow."

"Listen, missy, I know how to catch a turtle." Nick cupped his hands in the water and splashed Maddie playfully. They were standing in the shallows of Willow Lake, and as usual, Nick was trying to catch her a turtle. Since this was their first day as an official couple, he was determined to nab one. Unfortunately, he was having a terrible run of luck.

The temperature was still scorching, and the duo wasn't alone. Luckily for them, the two families and handful of teenagers who were visiting the lake opted to park in the lot across the watery expanse – so their little stretch of beach and water was mostly quiet.

Maddie had insisted on wearing a bathing suit, which turned out to be fortuitous. Most of the time, they had the lake to themselves. It was still open to the public, so it's not like Nick could ban visitors – as much as he wanted to. He was going to have to engage in his lake fantasy after dark, and later in the week, when they were assured of some alone time.

"You have to catch a turtle today," Maddie said.

"Why?" Nick crossed his arms over his sun-bronzed chest.

"Because I need to name it."

"What are you going to name it?"

"I can't tell you."

"If you name it Nick, we're breaking up."

Maddie put her hands on her narrow hips. "You know very well I already have a Nick turtle."

Nick waited a moment, and then he focused back on his task. "Don't you dare move, Maddie." He plunged his fingers into the water and then raised his hands triumphantly, the struggling red-eared slider scratching at his hands as he gripped it tightly. "Hah!"

Maddie clapped her hands excitedly, her braids bouncing up and down. "Yay!" As much as Nick liked her hair loose, he hadn't put up much of an argument when she wanted to braid her long locks before their lake outing. She'd explained about snarls, and how it would be painful to brush out later, and he'd relented. She was kind of cute with the twin braids anyway. He was constantly fighting the urge to tug on them so he could hold her still for a kiss.

He handed the turtle to an eager Maddie, and then watched as she ran her fingers over the painted shell. The turtle was angry, and he kept lashing out in an attempt to bite Maddie, but she was adept in her evasion. "Who's pretty?"

Nick pressed his lips together. "You think the turtle is pretty?"

"I think he's beautiful," Maddie said, petting him one more time and then lowering him back to the water. "Farewell, Mick."

Nick furrowed his brow. "Mick? Like Mick Jagger?"

Maddie shook her head.

Nick thought about it a moment and then grinned. "You combined our names. You turned us into a celebrity couple."

"No, I didn't," Maddie said evasively.

"Yes, you did."

She tried to skate around him when he reached for her, but he snagged her around the waist and twirled her around. "Admit it!"

"Fine. I named him after us."

Nick lowered her back to the ground but continued to hold her flush against his body. "And this is why I love you."

Maddie held up her hand, her fingers clasped around something. Nick took the Petoskey stone without question. He hadn't even seen her pick it up.

"For luck," Maddie whispered, rubbing her nose against his cheek.

"Oh, my Maddie," Nick sighed, kissing her deeply. "I'm already the luckiest man in the world."

The duo sank into their kiss, and they were well on their way to some mindless groping when the sound of someone clearing their throat on the shore caught their attention. Nick reluctantly pulled away, jerking slightly when he saw who was looking at them. "Kreskin."

"I'm sorry to interrupt," Kreskin said, eyeing the couple ruefully. "You'll never know how sorry I am."

"I thought we traded shifts," Nick said.

"We did. There's been a ... development."

Nick waited.

"We found a body this morning," Kreskin said.

"Where?"

"She was on the edge of the fairgrounds," Kreskin said. "She was under the same trees where Maddie was ... approached ... the other night."

Nick stiffened and pulled Maddie closer. "Who?"

"Tara Warner."

Maddie gasped, causing Nick to press his lips to the side of her face. "Shit. Give us a minute to pack up our stuff."

"I'm sorry," Kreskin said. "I didn't want to bother you, but I figured you'd want to know."

"No, you did the right thing," Nick said, pushing Maddie in front of him as they climbed out of the water.

Maddie immediately moved to the blanket where they'd set up their picnic and started pulling her clothes on while Nick waited beside Kreskin. "How did she die?" Nick asked.

"She was strangled."

"No one saw anything?"

"As far as I can tell, the last time anyone saw her was last night at the fair," Kreskin replied. "She was having fun near the dance floor."

"Was she alone?"

"She was with a group of women."

"Anyone I know?" Nick asked worriedly.

"Cassidy was there."

Nick sighed. "Well, at least we know she didn't actually kill her," he said.

"That's about all we know," Kreskin said. "The state police collected evidence this morning. I've been trying to find you. No one was at your house, or Maddie's house, and you weren't answering your phone."

Nick glanced around. "Sorry. It's in my shoe. I didn't hear it."

"I think you had your hands full with something else."

"Yeah," Nick said. "I certainly did. How did you find us?"

"I saw Maude downtown," Kreskin said. "By the way, she and Irma are dressed in camouflage to do something ... weird."

"They're stalking Harriet. She wants to be a Pink Lady. They're harmless."

"Maude told me where you were, but only after I explained how important it was to find you," Kreskin said. "She didn't want to tell me."

"It's fine," Nick said. "I want to solve this sooner rather than later. The longer we wait, the more danger Maddie is in."

"Do you want to drop her off back at the house?"

Nick shook his head. "We'll go back to the house long enough so you can sit downstairs while she showers and changes her clothes. I'll run out to my house and do the same, and pack enough so I don't have to leave her again. Then we'll all go to the scene."

"It will probably be pretty late by then. They're not shutting down the fair."

"I don't care," Nick said. "I don't want her alone. That means she's coming with me."

"Is she okay with that?"

Nick met Maddie's worried gaze behind Kreskin's back. "Yes. She needs to be with me. She won't complain."

"Okay, man. Let's go."

"SO, BREAK DOWN THE SCENE," Nick said.

It was two hours later, and he was standing next to Kreskin in the same spot he'd found Maddie on the ground two nights before. Maddie was hanging back, not far enough away to worry Nick, but not close enough to infringe on their investigation either.

"She was found here," Kreskin said, pointing. "She was on her back, and her ... skirt was hiked up above her waist. Her panties were gone, and she either wasn't wearing any or whoever was here took them as a souvenir."

"Was she raped?" Maddie asked, horrified.

"Fluids were found," Kreskin said carefully. "They're being rushed through the crime lab."

Maddie pressed her eyes shut to block out the image. "Oh."

"Mad, don't think about it," Nick instructed.

"Why doesn't she go to the fair?" Kreskin suggested. "We'll only be a few minutes, and then you two can enjoy the rest of your evening."

"No," Nick said immediately. "She's staying with me. I won't risk her leaving my side."

"Okay," Kreskin said, holding up his hands. "I'm sorry I suggested it."

"I'm not angry," Nick said. "I just want her with me."

"I get it," Kreskin said. "You just got her. You don't want to lose her."

"I won't ever lose her," Nick said. "Ever." He sucked in a steadying breath. "So, give me a timeline. When was she last seen at the fair?"

"Well, she was there when the Blackstone Boys were on the stage playing, and they were on between nine and ten."

Maddie wrinkled her nose. "The Blackstone Boys?"

"Leonard Sparks and his brothers have a band," Nick replied.

"They used to call themselves the Sparkly Boys, but then someone explained that probably wasn't a very manly name," Kreskin added.

Maddie forced a small smile onto her face, if only for Kreskin's benefit. "Oh."

"Anyway, she was at a table with several other women, including Cassidy and Marla Proctor," Kreskin said. "Just so you know, and I had to put it in the report so it's out there for public consumption, they were apparently plotting Maddie's downfall."

Nick stiffened. "Meaning?"

"It was nothing big," Kreskin said. "I believe there was some chatter about taking an ad out in the newspaper warning women to lock up their men. They were going to use a photograph of Maddie with it."

Nick scowled. "I'll talk to Beverly. She's been the editor at the newspaper for twenty years. She won't allow them to do anything of the sort."

"I know," Kreskin said. "I just thought you should know that they're plotting. I'm sure it will all be juvenile, but with Marla as the ringleader ... ."

"I hated that witch in high school," Nick grumbled. "I really hate her now." He cast a reassuring look in Maddie's direction. "It's going to be okay, Mad. She's just bitter."

"I know."

"Come here." Nick gestured for Maddie to come to him. When she was near, he pulled her into his arms and rested his head against her shoulder. "It's going to be all right."

"I'm hardly worried about Marla when Tara is ... ."

"I know," Nick said, brushing her hair down. "So, no one by the beer tent saw Tara slip into the trees?"

"No," Kreskin said. "Of course, the people hanging there aren't reliable witnesses. Most of the people staying close to the beer tent are the hardcore partiers. They wouldn't have noticed if aliens landed and probed them."

Maddie shifted in Nick's arms, surprised. "Wow. You're kind of funny."

"Sorry," Kreskin said. "This isn't a time to be funny. I just ... it kind of slipped out."

Maddie patted his arm. "I understand. You're a good man. Don't worry. I see it, so other people see it, too."

Kreskin smirked. "I see what Winters sees in you. If you weren't attached to his hip, I might make a play for you myself."

"You're married," Nick pointed out.

"Yeah, but she's something special." Kreskin winked at Maddie.

"She is," Nick agreed. "She's *my* something special. She could never fall for the likes of you."

Kreskin grinned. It was weak but heartfelt. "It's good you finally put him out of his misery and agreed to date him, Maddie," he said. "I don't know how long I could put up with his mopey face."

"His mopey face?"

"It's like Dopey, only sad."

Maddie nodded sagely. "I call it his puppy-dog face."

"Do you let him lick your face and cuddle up next to you when he gives you the look?"

"All right," Nick said, breaking up their banter. "We're at a murder scene."

Maddie instantly sobered. "I'm sorry."

Nick rubbed her shoulders absent-mindedly. "When was Tara's body discovered?"

"Not until the cleaning crew came in this morning," Kreskin said. "One of the guys came over here to ... relieve himself ... and he's the one who found her."

"What's her time of death?"

"All we know is between nine and midnight right now. It's a big window."

"Yeah," Nick agreed. "Well, why don't you go and get some sleep – or spend some time with your wife – or do whatever it is you want to do."

"What are you going to do?" Kreskin asked.

"I'm going to spend a few more minutes here, and then I'm going to buy my girl some junk food and then take her home and put her to bed. I might take her into the funhouse. We were supposed to do it the other night, but other things came up."

Kreskin looked surprised. "The funhouse? You don't strike me as a funhouse kind of guy."

"He claims the best memory of his life was in the funhouse," Maddie said dryly, moving away from Nick so she could look around the scene.

Kreskin arched an eyebrow.

"When we were seventeen, we were in the funhouse and Maddie got scared," Nick explained. "She threw herself in my arms and it was the first time I realized how big her boobs had gotten."

Kreskin snickered. "Nice."

"It was the best moment of my life," Nick said, shifting his gaze back to Maddie. "Until yesterday."

Kreskin clapped him on the back. "You're officially love whipped, boy. Enjoy it."

"I have every intention of enjoying it," Nick said.

"Keep her close," Kreskin added, lowering his voice and moving to leave the clump of trees. "She's kind of cute."

"She's totally cute," Nick said. "And, trust me, she's going to be right by my side for the rest of my life."

Kreskin grinned. "Good for you."

"Good for us."

21. TWENTY-ONE

Once Kreskin was gone, Nick focused on Maddie. "Is she here?"

Maddie raised a quizzical eyebrow. "Who?"

"Tara."

"Oh," Maddie said, realization washing over her. "That's why you wanted me here. You wanted to see if I could talk to Tara's ghost."

"I wanted you here because I can't bear to be away from you right now," Nick replied, earnest. "I want to touch you every second of the day, and I want to be able to see you every possible moment."

"Because of the danger, I know," Maddie said. "I didn't mean … ."

"Not just because of the danger, Mad," Nick said. "I just don't want to be away from you. My heart can't take it."

Maddie's stomach clenched. "You're so sweet."

"I love you. I finally get to say it, and I finally get to mean it, and I finally get to embrace it. I have no intention of leaving your side."

Maddie couldn't hide the tears that filled her eyes.

"If you cry, I'm going to be so upset," Nick said. "I don't want you to ever cry."

"Sometimes women cry because they're happy, not sad," Maddie explained.

"I know. I just ... if you cry, I'm going to cry. That's going to ruin my street cred."

Maddie made an exasperated sound in the back of her throat. "Fine. Just know, I'm going to think about this moment when we're alone tonight, and I'm going to cry then."

"If you hold off until then, I'll reward you with a back massage."

Maddie's face brightened. "Really?"

"Really," Nick said. "Now, focus on the scene. Can you ... I don't know ... see anything?"

"What do you want me to see?" Maddie asked, torn.

"How do you usually see things?"

"In my dreams." Maddie tilted her head to the side, considering. "And I didn't dream last night."

Nick swallowed hard. "Is it because you were with me?"

"No. I think it was because I was exhausted. No offense, sweetie, but the past few days have been emotionally draining."

"And physically draining because of your ankle," Nick said. "Shouldn't Tara's ghost be here?"

Maddie glanced around ruefully. "Even people who die under violent circumstances don't always come back as ghosts. Some are enlightened enough to just let it go."

"Well, that's disappointing."

"Not necessarily," Maddie said. "If Tara passed on, at least she not trapped here and suffering."

"That's not what I meant, Mad," Nick said hurriedly. "I was just hoping we could get some insight into what happened to her. She might know who killed her."

"It usually doesn't work like that, at least not right away," Maddie said. "Most ghosts take time to register the worst moment of their life. Dying is ... traumatic. Most souls want to forget it, so it takes them time to remember. Something usually jolts them."

"Tara's not here, though," Nick pointed out. "We don't even have the option of giving her the time to remember."

"Just because she's not here right now, that doesn't mean that she's not still here," Maddie said. "It's hard for them at first. They can't control when they pop up, or even where sometimes. Manifesting exhausts them.

"In fact, I haven't seen my mom in almost two weeks," she said, her voice cracking.

"Are you worried she's gone?"

"She wouldn't leave without saying goodbye," Maddie replied. "Granny is convinced she's staying until they can go together. I believe her."

"I'm sure she'll be back, love."

"That night, in the water, she appeared to me," Maddie said. "She was in the water, and she was trying to get me to swim. It was so cold, and I tried so hard, but I just couldn't make my body move. She kept telling me you were waiting for me."

Nick licked his lips. "I was waiting for you. I heard her that night, too."

Maddie was stunned. "What? Why didn't you tell me?"

"I don't know," Nick said. "It was weird. I wasn't sure I was hearing her. It was like a whisper. She was telling me how to find you. I don't know what you remember, but I parked on the road and went through the woods – even though I didn't know them – because something told me I had to get to you.

"It was like she was guiding me," he said. "I never made a wrong turn."

"That sounds like her," Maddie said, thoughtful. "If she expelled enough energy for you to hear her, that would explain why I haven't seen her. She's just regrouping. That makes me feel better."

"I heard her in the hospital, too," Nick said. "When I was sitting at your bedside, I heard her tell you that we were all there for you. Then I heard her whispering to Maude while she slept. I don't know what she said, but Maude was smiling in her sleep, so it must have been good."

"Granny told me she had a dream about Mom that night," Maddie said. "She said Mom told her we were about to go on an adventure. I chalked it up to Granny's imagination. She's never been able to talk to ghosts before. Now, though, I'm not so sure."

Nick grinned. "We are on an adventure, Mad," he said. "It's going to be the best adventure ever."

"Better than *The Goonies*?"

Nick nodded. "You have no idea how great it's going to be."

Maddie hugged him tightly, lifting her lips so he could give her a sweet kiss. "I love you, Nicky."

"I love you, my Maddie."

"I see you two finally managed to get together."

Maddie stilled in Nick's arms, swiveling quickly when she heard the voice. When her eyes landed on Tara's ghost, she was both heartbroken and relieved. "Tara."

"She's here?" Nick kept his voice low.

"So, in addition to being psychic, you can see ghosts, too, huh? That's handy," Tara said. Her face was drawn, her tone dark.

"I'm so sorry," Maddie said. "If I had seen this happening to you, I would have stopped it. I just didn't see." She slipped her hand into Nick's. "I don't know why I didn't see it."

"You saved me on the street, Maddie," Tara said. "I'm guessing I was supposed to die then. You did the best you could."

"It wasn't enough."

"You can't do everything, can you?"

"I guess not."

"I'm glad to see you and Nick finally found each other," Tara said. "He bought your flowers from me. Did you like them?"

"They were beautiful," Maddie said. "I didn't realize he bought them from you."

Nick's face was unreadable as he watched Maddie talk to air. He was comfortable letting her do her thing, which was the best gift he ever could have given her – even better than the turtle and the flowers.

"He was nervous," Tara said, smiling. "He was cute, though."

"He's always cute. Do you know what happened to you?"

"I'm not sure," Tara said. "We were listening to the band. I was getting a headache. There was only so much bitching I could put up with. Marla was really pushing Cassidy's buttons.

"You should know, I don't think every horrible thing Cassidy has done was her idea," she continued. "I didn't realize until last night that Marla was pulling her strings. She's been putting ideas in her head."

"That doesn't surprise me."

"Anyway, I needed a break," Tara said. "I volunteered to go to the beer tent. I remember talking to someone ... I think it was Alan. He was really drunk, and he wanted to dance. It was better than talking to Marla, so I told him after I dropped the drinks off at the table I would love to dance.

"The line was kind of long, and I was waiting in it, when ... I don't know ... it kind of goes black," she said. "I think something caught my attention in the trees. That's not really a memory. It's just something I think I know."

"It's okay," Maddie soothed. "You're doing great. What's the absolute last thing you remember?"

"Knowing that I'd made a terrible mistake."

Maddie swallowed hard. "Did you see who it was? Did you see his face? Can you describe him?"

Tara shook her head. "No."

"Did you get a feeling of familiarity? When you think about it, do you think you recognized him?"

"I don't know," Tara said. "I'm sorry."

"Don't worry," Maddie said. "Hopefully it will come back to you. You're probably not going to be able to stay here long. You've already expelled a lot of energy. When you come back, find me. Go ahead and come to the house. Granny knows everything, so I'll be able to talk to you without worrying about it."

"I see Nick knows, too," Tara said, fading slightly. "Is that why you left him when you were a teenager?"

"Yes."

"Did you think he wouldn't understand?"

"Yes."

"He's a better man than you gave him credit for," Tara said, almost invisible now.

"He's the best man in the world," Maddie said. "When you come back, find me."

"I will."

Once she was gone, Maddie exhaled heavily and turned to Nick. "She doesn't know who it was. The last thing she remembers is Alan asking her to dance. She thinks something grabbed her attention by the trees, but she's not sure what. She doesn't remember dying. I'm not sure I want her to."

"It's okay," Nick said, kissing Maddie softly. "It's okay."

Maddie wrapped her arms around his waist and basked in his warmth for a few minutes. "Can we get out of here? I don't want to be here anymore."

"Sure," Nick said, kissing her forehead. "Let's get some dinner because I don't want to cook and I don't want to order pizza again, and then we'll go. We'll watch a movie."

Maddie was intrigued. "What movie?"

"How about *The Goonies*?"

Maddie smiled. "That sounds ... perfect."

Nick linked his fingers with hers as they emerged from the trees. "As much as I'd like a repeat of the funhouse, I was thinking we could put it off until the next festival. It's Blackstone Bay, after all, and it will only be a few weeks before we get another chance."

"Thank you," Maddie said. "I just can't deal with that stuff right now."

"I can't either," Nick said, leading Maddie through the crowd. "You have to make me a promise, though."

"What promise is that?"

"You're going to let me feel you up when we finally get to go to the funhouse."

Maddie chortled. "Seriously?"

"I'm easily pleased."

"I promise."

Nick smiled. "So, what do you want to eat?"

"I want Middle Eastern from Paul's stand."

"The food is good," Nick agreed. "That sounds good. I'll buy you a kabob and some rice, and then we'll pick up elephant ears on the way out. I figured we could also get caramel corn, cotton candy, and ice-cream cones for the walk home."

"Do you want me to get sick?"

"No one says you have to eat it all," Nick reminded her.

"Yes, but you also know I have zero willpower. Why do you think I run five miles a day?"

"Because you know you look hot in those tiny shorts," Nick shot back.

"I've probably gained five pounds since I hurt my ankle," Maddie said.

"You're the most beautiful person in the world, Mad," Nick said. "Your body is amazing. Some junk isn't going to hurt it, at least for one night. I want junk food and you tonight. That's it."

"I guess you're going to get your wish," Maddie replied. "That's what I want, too."

"See, we really are perfect for each other." Nick stopped in the middle of the fair long enough to grace her with a smoldering kiss.

Maddie was happily encouraging him with her tongue when a voice interrupted their interlude.

"Oh, you two really have no shame, do you?"

Maddie moved to pull away from Nick, but he stilled her with a forceful arm around her waist. "What do you want, Marla?" he asked, irritated. "No one invited you to our personal party."

"This is a public fair," Marla said, tugging on Cassidy's arm and pulling the woman closer so they were standing shoulder to shoulder. "Are you two happy?" Maddie noticed that Charles was present again, although he was hanging back and staring at her rather than Marla.

"We are," Nick said. "You should try it. You'd be surprised how happiness eradicates the need to hurt others from your life."

"Oh, is that what you're doing?" Marla asked, sarcasm dripping from her tongue. "I thought you were rubbing your indiscretion in your ex-girlfriend's face."

Nick's was neutral as he regarded Cassidy. "I'm sorry to hurt you," he said. "I had no idea you'd be here. We didn't have plans to come, but Tara's death kind of threw our day into disarray."

"Oh, what a great apology," Marla said.

"Shut up, Marla," Nick snapped. "I'm not putting up with your crap tonight. We're getting food, and then we're leaving. Why don't you two go away for ten minutes, and then we'll be out of your hair."

"That would make things so much easier for you, wouldn't it?" Marla pressed. "Maybe Cassidy doesn't want to make your life easier. Right, Cassidy? You want to make them pay, don't you?"

Cassidy's face was so miserable, Maddie lost her breath for a moment. "I'm really sorry, Cassidy," she mumbled.

"You look sorry," Cassidy said. "All that pawing and kissing you were doing was clearly a heartfelt apology to me."

"You tell them, Cassidy," Marla said. "Put them in their place."

Cassidy opened her mouth and then snapped it shut. "I'm sure you two will get everything you deserve." She turned to leave, but Marla stayed her with a hand on her arm.

"Come on," Marla said. "Let them have it."

"Why? They've already got everything I want," Cassidy said, bitter. "Why would they possibly care about hurting me when they're so happy?"

"Cassidy, please don't ... ." Nick broke off, unsure.

"Don't do what?" Cassidy asked. "Tell the truth?"

"I'm sorry we hurt you," Nick said. "I'm not sorry I'm with Maddie, though. We weren't trying to be disrespectful. We're getting our dinner, and then we're leaving. The fair is officially yours."

Nick tugged on Maddie's hand. "Come on. I believe we have a movie in our future."

Maddie could feel Marla and Cassidy's eyes boring into her back as they left, but she didn't turn around. Charles' smile was enigmatic as they moved past him. "I see I was late to the game," he said, smiling widely. "I'm so disappointed."

Nick shot him a look. "You were a decade late to the game."

Maddie forced a smile onto her face as she let Nick lead her away. He was right. She was done apologizing for finally being happy. She had the one thing she'd always wanted. She wasn't going to give him up. Not again. Not ever.

22. TWENTY-TWO

"Tell me about Marla's boyfriend," Nick said the next morning over breakfast. He'd been curious the previous evening, but he'd refrained from asking in an effort to cajole Maddie back into a good mood. The exchange with Marla and Cassidy had drained her, and that was after a tense conversation with a ghost. All he'd wanted the night before was to wrap his body around hers and relax for a few hours before succumbing to sleep.

A new day was a new set of problems, though.

"His name is Charles," Maddie said. "Charles Hawthorne. He has a number after his name."

"Number?"

"Yeah, he's a third. Charles Hawthorne the third."

"Why is that important?" Nick was confused.

"It's not important to me, but it seemed to be a big deal to Marla," Maddie said.

"How do you know all this? Did it come up in your reading?"

"No. She volunteered it at Christy's salon."

"I thought she was banned from Christy's salon?"

"She was, but she came in on her hands and knees," Maddie said. "She was even nice to me for ten minutes because Christy threatened her with a shaved head if she wasn't. She was really excited about the date."

"Do you remember what Marla said he did for a living?"

Maddie shrugged, her morning hair tousled with sleep. "I don't know. I think she said he was an investment banker. I have no idea what that entails, but Marla seemed to think it was a big deal."

"It probably means he has money," Nick said, munching on his bowl of cereal thoughtfully. "He must have an important name and the pedigree to back it up. That's the only thing that would entice Marla. She's certainly not in the game for love."

Maddie played with a slice of banana in her cereal bowl. "What do you think about Cassidy?"

Nick didn't stop his chewing, but he did soften his eyes as he regarded Maddie. "I think she's sad."

"I feel horrible."

"I also think she's pathetic," Nick said. "No, don't argue with me. I'm sorry. I did not want to hurt her, but it was obvious where things were going. She purposely tried to drag things out to keep us apart, and she purposely tried to guilt us last night."

Nick captured Maddie's hand as it tapped on the top of the dining room table. "I love you, Maddie. Do you love me?"

"More than anything."

"Don't feel guilty about being happy," Nick said. "We're not reveling in Cassidy's sadness. We're just trying to be honest with one another. I will not put our happiness on hold because Cassidy is miserable."

"Still, it had to be like a punch in the gut for her to see us," Maddie said.

"That wasn't my plan, Mad," Nick said. "I had every intention of spending the day out at the lake – our lake – and then curling up with you and a book. I couldn't control Tara dying, and Cassidy is just going to have to accept that."

"I know," Maddie said. "I'm not sorry we're together. I'll never be sorry for that."

Nick squeezed her hand. "I'll never be sorry either. Now, eat your breakfast."

Maddie did as instructed.

Once they were both finished and standing next to the dishwasher so they could load it, Nick finally spoke again. "I need to go into the office today."

"I figured," Maddie said, straightening as she shut the front door of the machine. "Do you want me to come with you?"

"You can come with me," Nick said. "The problem is, I have no idea if I'll be out and about questioning people or stuck in a small room for eight hours."

"Okay." Maddie wasn't sure where he was going with the admission.

"What are you going to do today?"

"It's the last day of the fair," Maddie said. "I was thinking of going back to the flea market. I didn't get to see everything last time. I wouldn't go to the carnival, or anywhere I could run into Marla or Cassidy, but ... ."

Nick pursed his lips. "Can you stay here?"

"I ... sure."

Nick rolled his eyes. "That's not very convincing."

"It's fine," Maddie said. "There's some cleaning I can do. I thought I might ... I don't know ... clean out a few drawers and some space in the closet for your stuff. Not that you'll be here all the time," she added hurriedly. "Just so ... ."

"Maddie, I'm going to be here as often as I can," Nick said. "I don't want to be away from you for even one night. I thought we might split our time between here and my house. I plan on giving you drawers and closet space, too."

"Oh." Maddie was relieved.

Nick rolled his eyes. "You're a piece of work, Maddie Graves. You need to stop being surprised when I tell you I want to be with you. That's an argument for another time, though. For today, can you please stay here?"

Maddie nodded.

"Thank you," Nick said. He gave her a soft kiss.

When they parted, Maddie sent Nick a questioning look. "Why were you asking about Charles?"

"I saw the way he was looking at you last night," Nick replied. "Now, I know how you look – even if you don't – and I'm fully prepared to have to fight off thousands of suitors."

"Suitors?"

"Fine, dogs," Nick conceded. "There was just something ... off ... about him. He was trying to get you to dance the other night."

"I remember," Maddie said. "I didn't know you did."

"I remember anyone trying to step in and steal my girl," Nick said.

"I wasn't your girl then," Maddie reminded him.

"You've always been my girl, Mad."

Maddie grabbed the back of his neck and kissed him fiercely.

"Oh, good, you two have progressed to making out in the kitchen," Maude said, strolling into the room. "That's nice."

Maddie pulled back, surprised. "Granny ... ."

"Stop calling me that," Maude warned.

"Where have you been?" Nick asked. "Did you even come home last night?"

"I came home," Maude said. "I just came from upstairs. Where did you think I was?"

"I have no idea," Nick said. "It bothers me that I didn't hear you, though. It means I'm falling down on the job."

"You're a pain," Maude said. "You two are finally sleeping after weeks of torment. Give it a little time before you toss yourself on the railroad tracks. If it's any consolation, I was eavesdropping in the hallway for five minutes before I came in, too."

Nick made a face. "Why would that be a consolation?"

"Not for you, for me," Maude said. "I'm practicing my spying skills. Harriet Proctor is going down."

"Granny, do you know about Tara?" Maddie asked, worried.

Maude stilled. "I heard. I'm so sorry, Maddie girl. I know it must be killing you. You went out of your way to save her, and then she still died."

"It's important that you're careful," Nick warned. "Maddie has promised to stay here today. I want you to do the same."

"I have plans," Maude balked. "I can't break them. We're in a delicate stage of our operation."

"Do I even want to know what that is?" Nick asked.

Maude narrowed her eyes, considering. "Probably not."

"Is it illegal?"

"Not really."

"That's not an answer," Nick pointed out.

"It was an answer," Maude countered. "It might not have been the answer you were looking for, but it was still an answer."

"Maude," Nick growled.

"Nick," Maude matched his tone.

"Granny, will you promise to stay with at least one other person at all times while you're out doing ... whatever it is you're doing?" Maddie asked.

Maude nodded. "I promise. You don't have to worry about me. Focus all your energy on Maddie."

"I always do," Nick said. "Still, I happen to love you, too."

"Of course you do," Maude said, her eyes sparkling. "I'm downright lovable."

NICK FOUND Maddie asleep on her bed when he returned to the house late in the afternoon. He'd confiscated the spare key under the ceramic turtle when he climbed the porch, mentally chastising himself for not doing it sooner. Everyone in town knew where that key was, and not all of them were as trustworthy as he was.

Nick watched her slumber, her blonde hair spilling out on the pillow beneath her and felt his heart swell. He didn't know it was possible to love anything as much as he loved Maddie.

He lowered himself onto the bed next to her carefully, smiling when she shifted and folded herself into his arms. "Nicky," she murmured.

"Maddie," he said, pressing a kiss into her hair. "My Maddie."

He joined her in sleep a few minutes later, his heart bursting with the love he'd been forbidden to express for a decade.

WHEN M**ADDIE WOKE AN HOUR LATER**, she was surprised to feel a strong body draped over hers. "Nicky?"

"Hello, love," he murmured, brushing his lips against her neck. "You're so warm."

Maddie rubbed her eyes, trying to get her bearings. "When did you get back?"

"About an hour ago."

"Why didn't you wake me up?"

"Because you looked like an angel," Nick said, pulling her tight against him. "You don't wake a sleeping angel. It's bad luck."

"You're making that up," Maddie teased.

"No, I'm not. How was your day?"

"I cleaned, and I read, and then I fell asleep. I have no idea why I was so tired. I've slept better the past two nights than I have in ... ten years."

"That's why you slept, love," Nick said. "You're finally happy."

"I am happy," Maddie agreed. "I still feel guilty."

Nick groaned and rolled on his back as he pinched his nose. "Because of Cassidy?"

"No, because of Tara."

Nick sighed. "We can't go back in time and save her," he said. "I know it's hard, and I know it's terrible, but it is what it is. We can only move forward. I have to keep you safe, Mad. That's what I'm focused on right now."

"Did you find anything out about Charles?"

Nick stiffened beside her. "I did."

"It doesn't sound like you found out anything good," Maddie said, rolling so she could rest her head on his chest.

Nick ran his fingers through her hair and studied her face. "Charles Hawthorne doesn't exist."

Maddie furrowed her brow. "How is that possible? He's a third. He has to exist."

"I found a few Charles Hawthornes," Nick said. "None of them was a third, and none of them look like that guy."

Maddie propped herself up on her elbow. "What does that mean?"

"Nothing good," Nick said. "There are a couple of possibilities."

"I'm waiting?"

Nick kissed her softly. "We don't have to talk about it now."

"I need to know."

Nick sighed. "He could be a conman. He might be going after Marla for money. She's not rich, by any stretch of the imagination, but the Proctor family has money. He might be a grifter."

Maddie mulled the idea over. "When he wanted me to read his cards, he asked if he was going to be rich forever. They didn't believe I was a real psychic, and when I looked at his cards, they were a mess. Instead of taking the time to actually read them, I made up a lie."

"What did you tell him?"

"That he was going to be rich forever."

"What did Marla want to know?"

"If he was going to be rich forever."

Nick barked out a laugh. "That's typical. What did you tell her?"

"That they deserved each other," Maddie replied. "He made me uncomfortable. I thought it was just because he was a letch, but what if it was something more?"

"I don't know," Nick said. "I honestly don't know, Mad. Focusing on Charles might be a mistake. He could just be after Marla's money."

"That's still illegal."

"It's not my concern, though," Nick said. "If Marla gets screwed over, that's karma."

"What if someone kills her?"

Nick sighed. "Well, that's a different story. We don't know enough to accuse Charles."

"So, what's your next step?"

"I need to try and get his fingerprints," Nick replied honestly.

"How are you going to do that?"

Nick shrugged. "I have no idea. It's the last night of the fair. I'm thinking he might be there with Marla. If I can get my hands on a beer glass ... ."

"You're going to the fair?"

"I don't see a lot of other options right now."

"Okay," Maddie said, resigned. "I guess I'll stay here."

"No," Nick said, immediately shaking his head. "It's the fireworks. We're going together. You can't miss the fireworks. You love them."

"What about Cassidy?"

"I already called Christy," Nick said. "You two are going to watch the fireworks together, and I'm going to go back and forth trying to get Charles' fingerprints. Kreskin is in on the plan, too."

"Really?"

Nick smiled. "Really. You and Christy can sit far enough on the outskirts not to draw attention, and I promise to be right by your side during the fireworks display. We can have the best of both worlds tonight."

"I don't want to get in the way of your job."

"You're never in my way," Nick said, kissing her quickly. "You might see Tara, and Christy will be the perfect alibi if you do."

"I see you've thought this all out."

"I have," Nick said. "I've also built in fifteen minutes so I can kiss your lips bloody before we have to get ready and go."

Maddie arched an eyebrow. "Oh, really?"

Nick made a show about checking his watch. "Yup. It starts now." He rolled over on top of her. "Prepare to beg for mercy."

"I don't want your mercy," Maddie teased.

"What do you want?"

"Kiss me."

"Finally, something I want to do."

Nick pulled Maddie close, lost in her eyes and the feel of her body as she melted into him. If he'd been more aware of his surroundings, he would have noticed a shadow in the hallway.

Maude had heard everything he said to Maddie, and she was formulating a plan of her own. Maddie's happiness was the most important thing in the world to Maude, and if she could help Nick with a task ... well ... that might be fun.

23. TWENTY-THREE

"Are you guys okay with this spot?" Nick asked.

"It's good," Christy said. "We're close enough to be around people, but far enough away where we won't have to risk Marla coming by. She'll want to be in the center of the action. She likes to torture Maddie, but she needs everyone looking at her even more."

Nick spread out a blanket on the ground and nudged the picnic basket to the edge of the blanket. "There's beer in there, and I'll bring you junk food back if you want it. It will be easier if I have tasks when I'm going back and forth. That way I won't look suspicious."

"You're very alpha tonight," Christy teased, settling on the blanket. "You're like a bundle of energy."

Nick fixed her with a look. "I'm trusting you to keep my Maddie in your sights at all times this evening."

Christy mimed a shocked face. "I think that's beyond my wheelhouse. However will I manage the impossible task you've set in front of me?"

"I'm not joking," Nick said.

"I've got it, Nick," Christy said. "We're going to sit on a blanket. You're going to bring us junk food. We're going to watch the fireworks. I'll be with her the whole night. You have nothing to worry about."

"I'm sorry," Nick said. "I just ... I need her to be safe."

"I get it, Mr. Macho," Christy said. "I won't let the love of your life out of my sight. I promise. Chill out. You're going to be making fifteen-minute loops. We're going to be sitting right here and gossiping."

Nick wasn't convinced. "What happens if one of you has to go to the bathroom?"

"I'm not answering that question," Christy said. "If I do, I'll say something inappropriate. Then Maddie will get embarrassed, and you're going to get turned on."

Maddie blushed furiously, while Nick smirked. "Just watch my girl, and while you're at it, watch yourself."

Nick tugged on a strand of Maddie's hair as he pulled her closer. "Be good, okay?"

"Be safe," Maddie said.

Nick pulled an item out of his pocket so Maddie could see it. The Petoskey stone turtle she'd bought him a few days before stared back at her from his palm. "I have luck on my side."

Maddie smiled. "You kept it?"

"I've kept them all, Maddie. You gave them to me. I'd never give them up." He gave her a quick kiss. "Have fun. I'll bring you food the next time I come around."

Once he was gone, Christy fixed Maddie with a sly smile. "Oh, Ken and Barbie have finally found their way together." She pressed her hand to her heart, mocking. "It's so sweet."

Maddie frowned. "We don't look like Ken and Barbie."

"You look exactly like Barbie," Christy said. "Nick looks more like the modified Ken, the one they introduced in the eighties with the brown hair. Unfortunately, neither version was anatomically correct."

"You're not funny."

"I'm very funny," Christy said. "And you're happy."

Maddie's pressed her lips together. "I ... is it that obvious?"

"You're practically glowing, Maddie," Christy said. "Nick is walking around with his chest all puffed out. The sex must be really, really good."

"We haven't had sex yet."

Christy was horrified. "Why not? You two have been waiting for more than a decade to do it. You need to do it, and then you need to tell me about it because I'm dying for details."

"Nick wants to wait for a little bit."

"Why?"

"He says he thinks I'm feeling too much pressure about it, and he wants us to be able to spend some time together before that's an issue," Maddie explained. "He wants to wait for two weeks."

"He actually set a timetable? That's ... cute ... I guess. What do you want?"

"I don't know," Maddie said. "I'm a little relieved, to tell you the truth. I don't have a lot of experience – not like he does – and it feels good just to be able to touch him whenever I want."

Christy's face softened. "He really does know you. He knew you weren't ready. He wants you to be comfortable with him on every level."

"I am comfortable with him on every level," Maddie protested.

"Yes, but you're discovering new levels every day," Christy said. "You have no idea what he's doing for you."

"What's he doing for me?"

"If I know Nick, he wants to make sure that all of this ... danger ... is settled and you're both relaxed before you take the biggest step of your lives," Christy said. "I'll bet he makes it special. Candles. Wine. Sensual music. He's kind of a romantic."

"He is," Maddie conceded.

"So, if you're not having sex, what are you doing?"

"Last night we cuddled up in bed and watched *The Goonies*," Maddie said.

"Oh, it's like you really are dating in high school now."

"And then we kissed for a few hours."

"Better," Christy said. "Is he a good kisser?"

"He's magic."

"I think the two of you together are magic," Christy said. "Enjoy it,

Maddie. You two have been waiting a lifetime for this. You don't have to rush anything. Just let it happen when it's supposed to happen."

"HERE YOU GO," Nick said, lowering the box of goodies onto the blanket and sitting down between Maddie and Christy. "What have you two been doing?"

"Well, Maddie told me you kiss like a rock star and you've put an embargo on sex," Christy said, smiling widely.

Nick grinned. "Really?" He arched an eyebrow in Maddie's direction. "A rock star, huh?"

Maddie made a face. "Don't get too excited. When I look at you, I see Nickelback."

Nick feigned a chest wound. "Oh, you know just how to hurt me." He leaned over and gave her a quick kiss. "I'll rock your mouth later."

"Have you managed to get Charles' fingerprints yet?" Christy asked, leaning back on her elbows.

"Kreskin is over there watching him now."

"Don't you think that Charles will find that suspicious?" Christy asked.

"Kreskin is with his wife, and they're watching the band," Nick said. "As far as anyone can tell, he's just enjoying a nice night at the fair."

Maddie perked up. "I want to meet his wife."

"She wants to meet you, too," Nick said. "We're all going out to dinner in the near future. I promised."

"She wants to meet me? Why?"

"Because Kreskin told her I was acting like a lovesick puppy who finally found his bone," Nick said, his tone dry. "She's dying to meet the bone."

"So is Maddie," Christy said, snickering.

"You have a filthy mind," Nick said. "You leave my Maddie alone. Don't push her into anything."

"Hey, I'm the one who told her how lucky she is because you

know her so well," Christy countered. "I'm on your side. You just need to learn how to take a joke."

Nick flicked the end of her nose. "I think you're actually good for her. You don't let her spend too much time in her own head. She's never had a female friend she wasn't related to before."

"I know. It's sad. Her whole childhood was you. The horror."

Nick smirked. "I still like you around her."

"You know I'm right here, don't you?" Maddie was exasperated.

"I could never forget your presence, love," Nick said. "Here. I got you a hot dog, fries, and an elephant ear. I got Christy chicken strips and fries."

"Hey, I like a good hot dog," Christy deadpanned.

"That's the word on the street," Nick teased right back. He handed Maddie her hot dog. "I left the onions off."

"I guess I'll survive," Maddie said, taking a huge bite out of the hot dog. Nick leaned forward and took a bite of it from the other end. "Hey! I'm hungry," Maddie said.

"That's why I got two."

"I may overdose on the sweetness," Christy grumbled.

Nick shot her a look. "I have to go back over there. Kreskin is going to signal me when Charles finishes a drink. We're going to try and get Kreskin's wife to pick up the glass so it's not too suspicious. Then we just have to bag it, and we're good to go."

"It's like a television show," Maddie said.

"Yes, it's like *Hawaii Five-o*," Christy said. "Only instead of defusing a bomb you're stealing a red solo cup."

"Okay," Nick said, pushing himself to his feet and glaring at Christy. "You need to start drinking. Otherwise, I'm going to have to gag you." He kissed the top of Maddie's head. "I'll be back in time for the fireworks."

"GRANNY, WHAT ARE YOU DOING?"

Maude was so enthusiastic when she approached the blanket she bowled Maddie over. "Sorry," she said, huffing out a raspy breath. "I just got over stimulated."

That was a frightening thought. "What are you doing?" Maddie asked, looking her grandmother up and down. The woman was dressed completely in black, and she had leather gloves on – which seemed to signify she'd been up to no good. "Harriet's not locked in a car trunk somewhere, is she?"

Maude made a face. "No. That's a great idea, though. How long do you think she could last in a trunk in this heat?"

Maddie extended a finger in Maude's direction. "Don't you dare!"

Maude rolled her eyes dramatically. "You need to learn how to take a joke, Maddie girl."

"That's what I've been telling her," Christy said.

"That's because you're a good friend," Maude said. "Oh, here, I brought you a present." Maude pulled a plastic baggie with a cup enclosed inside out of her purse and handed it to Maddie.

"What's this?"

"It's Charles Hawthorne's cup."

Maddie's mouth dropped open. "What? How? What?"

"I heard you and Nick in the bedroom earlier," Maude said. "You need to start shutting your door, by the way. Once you two get beyond the groping and kissing phase, I'm going to be scarred for life if I see the big event."

"So am I," Maddie griped. "Where did you get this?"

"From Charles," Maude said, shrugging.

"How?"

"Well, Irma distracted him by rubbing her boobs against the back of his head, and then I pretended I needed a drink and I took the cup," Maude said. "It wasn't hard."

"Granny, Nick and Kreskin are over there trying to get this cup right now," Maddie said. "You've totally ruined their operation."

"You mean I did their job for them," Maude corrected. "Tell them I'll accept payment in the form of scratch-off lottery tickets or public accolades."

Christy chortled while Maddie furrowed her brow. "Granny, Nick is going to be mad."

"Why? I put it in a baggie. I followed the procedure from *CSI*."

"I don't think Nick is going to see it that way."

"Well, then kiss him until he does," Maude said, unruffled. "He seems addicted to your lips right now. You've got power over him."

"Granny," Maddie groaned.

"He's heading this way," Christy said, pointing.

Maude straightened. "I need to run. I'm too pretty for prison." She wagged her finger in Maddie's face. "You make him see I did him a favor, and don't you bother coming home until you do."

Maude hopped off of the blanket and bolted into the night.

Nick was scowling when he reached Maddie and Christy.

"How did it go?" Christy asked brightly.

"I have no idea what happened," Nick said. "The cup was there, and then suddenly it wasn't. Now we have to start all over again."

Maddie worried her bottom lip with her teeth. "Um ... no you don't."

"What do you mean?"

Maddie handed him the plastic bag. Nick furrowed his brow as he studied it.

"What is this?"

"Charles' cup."

"How did you get it?" Nick asked suspiciously.

"I ... ."

"Maude stole it," Christy supplied. "What? I'm not going to sit here and watch you get in trouble because you don't want to rat out your grandmother, Maddie."

"How did she even know to get it?"

"Apparently she was eavesdropping on you two while you were rolling around on Maddie's bed," Christy replied. "You're going to want to shut the door from now on, by the way. Maude is terrified she's going to bear witness to the actual deed at some point."

"We're all terrified of that," Nick grumbled. "I can't believe she did this. Do you have any idea what this means?"

"You got outsmarted by a senior citizen?" Christy suggested.

Nick scowled. "It means we can't use the fingerprints for a conviction if Charles happens to be guilty. We can't prove the chain of custody for the fingerprints."

Maddie's face fell. "Oh."

"It's not like you did it, Mad," Nick said, shoving the plastic bag and cup into the picnic basket to hide it from prying eyes. "I am going to kill her. You know that, right?"

"She says we can't come home until you forgive her."

"I'd like to see her stop me."

"If it's any consolation, she was wearing black gloves," Christy said brightly.

Nick ignored her and settled behind Maddie, spreading his legs so he could cuddle up behind her. "It's not any consolation."

Christy knit her eyebrows together. "Are you going to pout the rest of the night?"

"Nope."

"How long are you going to pout?"

"Five minutes."

"Okay," Christy said, getting to her feet. "I'm going see if I can find a man on the dance floor. You two enjoy the rest of your night."

"You're leaving?" Maddie asked, disappointed.

"I think you two should enjoy your first fireworks display as a couple alone," Christy said. "Trust me. I have no inclination to watch you two make out for the next hour."

"We won't," Maddie protested. "I don't want you to feel like we're forcing you out. Tell her, Nicky."

"I'm going to kiss her until she can't breathe." Nick's face was serious.

Christy grinned. "I figured. Have fun."

"Wait," Nick said as she started to move away. "Don't walk home alone. Be careful."

Christy saluted. "Yes, sir."

"Christy?"

"Yeah."

"Thank you for keeping her safe." Nick kissed Maddie's cheek.

"Thank you for putting a smile on her face," Christy said, brushing the seat of her pants off. "I can't wait to see what she's like when you two finally get naked together."

"Me either," Nick said, wrapping his arms around Maddie's waist. "I'm happy with this smile for now, though."

24. TWENTY-FOUR

"What are you going to do today?" Nick asked, rubbing his hand over Maddie's flat abdomen as they cuddled in bed together the next morning.

"Well, the fair is over, so I'll probably just stick close to home today."

"Are you just saying that because you think it's what I want to hear?"

"I'm saying it because I should probably open the store today. It is a business, after all."

Nick nuzzled his nose against Maddie's cheek. "I forgot you own a business. I thought that was just the room that decorated our window seat."

Maddie giggled. "I made a lot of money running the tent, so that's good. Still, it would be nice to get some actual customers into the store for a change."

"You'll be careful when people come into the store, right?"

"You know I managed to survive for twenty-eight whole years before we got together, don't you?"

"Don't remind me."

"What are you going to do today?"

"Well, Kreskin dropped the cup off at the office and uploaded the prints last night," Nick said. "Hopefully it won't take too long to find out who Charles Hawthorne really is."

"I have a question," Maddie said.

"Yes, I love you."

"I have another question."

"No, no one is more handsome than me."

Maddie snorted. "I have one more question, and I want to actually ask it before you say something cute."

"Well, you'd better hurry up," Nick said, brushing his lips against the corner of her mouth. "I have fifteen minutes before I have to get in the shower, and I want to kiss you for all of them."

"What happens if Charles Hawthorne doesn't show up in the system?"

Nick stilled. "Then we start over from scratch."

"Does that mean you'll be staying here indefinitely?"

"Why, am I getting on your nerves?"

"No. I just ... I don't want to deal with having to sleep without you when you finally decide I'm not in danger any longer," Maddie admitted.

"What makes you think you'll have to sleep without me?"

"I don't know," Maddie said. "I just figure you'll want to sleep in your own bed sometimes."

"Are you allergic to my bed?"

"No."

"Is there a reason you can't sleep in my bed with me?"

"No."

"Then what's the problem?"

"Are you sure you want me to sleep with you in your bed?"

Nick groaned. "Maddie, I want you next to me every night. Whether we sleep in your bed, or my bed, we're going to be sleeping together."

"Are you sure? I don't want to crowd you. I know you like your space."

"Who told you that?"

"Christy says you only went out twice a week with the women you were seeing while I was gone," Maddie said. "What if you get tired of me?"

"First off, Christy has a big mouth," Nick said. "Second, why do you think I only wanted to see those women twice a week?"

"Because you value your privacy."

"I do like a little alone time, but that's not why," Nick said, smiling. "You know I only dated those women because I didn't think I could have you, right?"

Maddie furrowed her brow, unsure.

"Maddie, I didn't want to spend too much time with those women because I knew I wasn't going to get attached to them and I didn't want them getting attached to me," Nick said. "I'm already attached to you, and I'm hoping you're already attached to me."

"I'm so attached to you it hurts when you're away."

Nick smiled. "Me, too. I'm not going to get tired of you, Maddie. Ever. I need you to stop thinking that. It freaks me out."

"I just don't want to do anything that will drive you away."

"Do you know what's going to drive me away?"

Maddie bit her lip and shook her head.

"Nothing." Nick pressed his lips against hers and rolled on top of her, pinning her beneath his weight. Once he had her exactly where he wanted her, he forced her to meet his gaze. "You're stuck with me forever, Maddie."

Maddie sucked in a breath. "I love you."

"I love you more than anything in this world." Nick kissed her again, this one lingering and soft. "Never forget that."

"SO, did you talk to Maude about her little adventure last night?" Kreskin asked Nick a few hours later as they caught up near the coffee pot in the small kitchenette at the police station.

"No. She didn't come home until we were already asleep, and she was gone before we got up this morning."

"How do you know she came home?"

"Her black gloves were on the kitchen counter, and she left a note for Maddie saying she'd catch up with her later – when the fuzz wasn't around to dampen her buzz."

Kreskin barked out a laugh. "That woman is a pip."

"She means well," Nick said. "She's just ... out there."

"Aren't you worried Maddie is going to end up just like her?"

"No. Why? You don't think Maddie will turn out like Maude, do you?"

"Does that scare you?"

Nick mulled the question over. "Not really. The only thing that scares me is losing Maddie."

"Do you think she's going to run away from you?"

Nick shrugged noncommittally.

"Let me tell you something, Winters," Kreskin said. "That woman loves you. You can see it in the way she looks at you. She can't get enough of you. I know you guys have some history where she left you and went to college, but she's home now. She's not going anywhere. You can't smother her because you're scared to lose her."

"Do you think I'm smothering her?"

"I think you two are in that heady infatuation phase at the beginning of every relationship where you don't want to be away from each other," Kreskin said. "Everyone goes through it, and it's normal. That's not what I was talking about, though."

"What were you talking about?"

"You can't wrap her in bubble wrap and protect her from everything," Kreskin said. "She's an adult, and she's proven she can take care of herself."

"She almost drowned."

"But she didn't," Kreskin said. "I understand wanting to keep her safe, especially given the fact that she's had two interactions with what is probably a cold-blooded killer. You can't watch her twenty-four hours a day, though. You have to have faith that she's capable of taking care of herself."

"I just can't bear the thought of someone hurting her," Nick admitted.

"I know. She's going to have to fight her own battles, though, and that includes with Marla and Cassidy. You can't step in the middle of a girl fight. You'll just get your eyes scratched out."

"The problem is, Marla isn't a girl. She's a bird of prey, and she's just waiting for the opportunity to peck Maddie to death. She's always fixated on Maddie."

"Because she's jealous of her?"

Nick nodded. "Maddie doesn't see it that way, but that's exactly why."

"Well, the good news is, Maddie has back-up from Christy Ford," Kreskin said. "If anyone can take Marla Proctor down, it's Christy. You have to let them handle it, though."

"What makes you think I won't?"

"Because right now, you can't think of anything but stepping between Maddie and any insult or hurt thrown her way," Kreskin said. "Listen, it's natural. When you love someone, you don't want anything bad to touch them. You just have to realize it's not possible to protect one person all of the time."

Nick rubbed the heel of his hand against his forehead. "I know. I just ... I love her."

"I've known that since the first time I saw you two together," Kreskin said. "There was a dead body in the alley, and all you could think about was the shaken blonde at the scene. Your girlfriend was staring daggers into your back, and yet you were fixated on Maddie.

"You know, even though I'm an outsider here, even I've heard the legend of you and Maddie," he continued. "When I first met you, I had a hard time reconciling the stories of your great lost love with a guy who dated on a schedule."

Nick scowled.

"I see it now," Kreskin said. "Maddie is different. She's special. She's your other half. You can love her and still give her room to grow."

"I just want her to be happy."

"I saw you two at the lake the other day," Kreskin said. "I don't think I've ever seen a woman look happier."

Nick smirked. "Thanks."

"Okay, I officially declare an end to any relationship advice for the foreseeable future," Kreskin said, patting Nick's shoulder. "How about we go check and see if we can find out who Charles Hawthorne really is?"

"That sounds good," Nick said. "I'm ready to solve this so Maddie and I can have a little room to breathe."

"Last time I checked, your idea of breathing was sucking all the oxygen out of her lungs through her mouth," Kreskin teased.

"Hey, that's still breathing."

MADDIE WAS LOST IN THOUGHT – and an organizing task – when the bell above Magicks jingled to signify an incoming customer. She glanced up, half expecting to see Maude slinking in, but the man standing in front of the door wasn't one she recognized.

"Can I help you?"

The man was handsome, an amiable smile and bright eyes offsetting a square jaw. He was in his forties, and he was dressed down in blue jeans and a basic T-shirt. "You're Maddie Graves, right?"

"Yes."

"I'm sorry, I don't think I've had a chance to introduce myself," the man said, stepping forward. "I'm Sheldon Higgins."

Recognition dawned on Maddie. "Oh, you're the mayor."

Sheldon nodded enthusiastically. "I am. I've been wanting to introduce myself, but I've just been so busy. I usually like to host a special event when a new business opens, and I've really fallen down on the job where you're concerned."

"Technically, I didn't open a new business," Maddie said, filing the final two books she was organizing onto a shelf, and then getting to her feet. "I just reopened my mom's shop. It's not a big deal."

"It's a big deal to me," Sheldon said. "I've just gotten behind with two festivals, and the other ... stuff. I came to apologize, and I was hoping we could set up a special event to highlight the store, maybe a theme night or something."

"Oh, that's really nice," Maddie said. "It's not necessary, though."

"I insist," Sheldon said.

"Well, I guess," Maddie hedged. "Do you want some iced tea? There's a calendar in the kitchen. We can pick out a day."

"That sounds great," Sheldon said.

"WE HAVE good news and bad news," Kreskin said, studying the computer screen.

"What's the good news?" Nick asked. "Tell me you know who Charles Hawthorne really is."

"He is in the system. His real name is Charles Harper."

"What's on his record?"

"He's an investment banker from Boston," Kreskin said. "He cleaned out three hundred clients and disappeared about a year ago with more than five million dollars in their money."

"I don't think most white color criminals suddenly jump to murder," Nick said.

"I agree. This guy is a criminal, he's just not the criminal we're looking for."

"Was that the bad news?" Nick asked.

"No," Kreskin said. "I also inputted the parameters of Tara Warner's death into the national database while we were waiting for the DNA results to come through. I was hoping it would be similar to other crimes, whether in the state or out, and I got a hit."

"Where?"

"Flint."

"What happened?"

"Another woman there was strangled and raped about eleven years ago," Kreskin said. "She was young and pretty, and witnesses said they saw a man in a dark hoodie in the area where the body was found. They never identified a suspect, but they did log the semen found."

"And?"

"It's a match for our semen," Kreskin said. "I compared the two samples manually."

"You're kidding."

"No," Kreskin said.

"Two victims. That makes him a serial killer," Nick said, his eyes thoughtful.

"The semen has multiple hits from fifteen years ago in Detroit, too," Kreskin said. "No one died in those cases, but a man did break into first-floor apartments in a rundown portion of the city. His features were hidden by a hoodie, and he brutally raped another five women."

"So, he escalated to murder eleven years ago," Nick mused. "Where has he been since then?"

"That's a very good question."

"SO, I don't know much about you," Maddie said, sitting in one of the chairs at the dining room table and pushing a glass of iced tea in front of Sheldon. "Where did you live before you moved to Blackstone Bay?"

"I've lived in a lot of different places," Sheldon said. "I spent some time down in Detroit, and then I lived in Flint for a year or so."

"What made you decide to come to Blackstone Bay?"

"Honestly? I was up here on vacation, and I just happened across the town," Sheldon said. "I loved it here. Two weeks after returning home, I just decided to move. I figured I might as well live in a town I loved since I didn't have anything anchoring me to Flint. I made the decision, and I moved five days later."

"Wow. That's brave."

"I don't think it's brave," Sheldon scoffed, shooting Maddie a winning smile. "It was more like destiny. Tell me about you, though. You grew up here and then moved down south for ten years?"

"I did."

"Did you come home because of your mother's death?"

"Partially," Maddie said. "I was ready to come home before Mom died, but once it happened, I knew someone had to take care of Granny."

"She is ... something," Sheldon said. "Is she the only reason you came home?"

"I came home for a lot of reasons."

"Was Nick Winters one of them?"

Maddie faltered. "I ... yes."

"It's a small town," Sheldon said. "Everyone talks. You and Nick are a constant source of gossip these days."

"I know," Maddie said. "Trust me. I know."

"I think it's sweet," Sheldon said. "Childhood love transcends time and blossoms in adulthood. It's like a fairy tale."

"I guess it kind of is."

Sheldon got to his feet. "Do you think I could use your restroom?"

"Oh, of course," Maddie said. She pointed over her shoulder. "It's the third door down on the left."

"Thank you," Sheldon said. "I'll be back in a few minutes, and then we'll talk about your special event."

"Great."

The second Sheldon left the room, Olivia popped into view. Her shape was faint, but her presence was welcome. "Mom," Maddie whispered. "I was worried. I didn't know how long it would be until I saw you again."

"We can catch up later, sunshine," Olivia said. "Now you have another problem."

"What problem? Is something wrong with Granny?"

"Maddie, you have to get out of this house right now."

"What? Why?"

"Because your guest is dangerous," Olivia hissed, her form dissolving even further.

"What do you mean?"

"I don't have time, Maddie," Olivia said. "I don't have the strength yet. Run. Run fast. Run now."

Olivia disappeared.

Maddie got to her feet, shaky. "Mom?"

"Were you talking to someone?"

Maddie froze when she heard Sheldon's voice behind her. She was in trouble. Again.

25. TWENTY-FIVE

"If Charles Hawthorne isn't our murderer, who is?" Nick asked, rubbing the back of his neck irritably.

"Well, let's think about it," Kreskin said. "What do we have to go on?"

"We have a timeline between Detroit and Flint," Nick suggested. "Who is an outsider here that we know lived in Flint?"

Kreskin furrowed his brow. "What about the mayor?"

Nick stilled.

"I was joking," Kreskin said.

"What about the mayor?" Nick pressed. "He's been here about ten years. He was in Flint eleven years ago. I have no idea where he was before that, but he's worth a shot."

"Have you met that guy? He's far too happy to be a murderer."

"Maybe it's an act," Nick suggested. "Or maybe he's on medication."

Kreskin was surprised by the suggestion. "We were wondering why someone would kill someone and then just stop for eleven years. What if he is on some kind of medication?"

"He was in the flower shop talking to Tara the other day," Nick said, his mind wandering.

"How do you know that?"

"I went in to buy flowers for Maddie. My mom said I couldn't tell her I loved her without flowers."

"Were those the flowers she was cradling on her chest in that window seat?"

Nick nodded.

"So, that was the day the flowers appeared on her front stoop, right?"

Nick nodded again.

"That was the afternoon before Tara died," Kreskin finished.

"Exactly."

"Well, crap," Kreskin said. "Let's run the mayor. I just have a feeling this is going to be a massive cluster of sludge."

"Run him," Nick said, suddenly feeling antsy. "Run him now. Tara said something about him coming in every week. She felt uncomfortable around him."

"WERE YOU TALKING TO SOMEONE?"

Maddie swiveled slowly, plastering a fake smile on her face as she regarded Sheldon with what she hoped was a welcoming expression. As a child, when she lied, Maude said she always knew because Maddie looked crazy. Maddie could only hope she'd outgrown that little quirk. "You caught me," she said. "When I'm organizing in my head, I often talk to myself."

"Oh, I think we all do that," Sheldon said. He was standing in the archway between the hallway and the kitchen. His face was still placid, but now Maddie saw something sinister lurking in the depths of his green eyes.

"Let me just grab the calendar," Maddie said, shuffling around the counter. It wasn't much of a safety net, but it was something at least. "It's in the drawer over here." Maddie opened the knife drawer and gripped the large butcher knife inside. She didn't brandish it, and she didn't make a move to take a step back. She just waited.

"You know, there are rumors about you," Sheldon said, shifting from one foot to the other.

"Oh, really?" Maddie raised an eyebrow. "What kind of rumors?"

"People say you're really psychic."

Maddie shook her head. "No. I just play one on television," she quipped lamely.

"People also say you talk to ghosts."

"What people say that?"

"It's just a whisper around the town," Sheldon said, being careful to keep his distance and refrain from any sudden moves.

"Well, you should know that gossip in Blackstone Bay isn't always reliable," Maddie said.

"I think this tidbit is," Sheldon said. "Do you want to know why?"

Not really, Maddie thought. "Sure."

"A dead woman told me."

Maddie faltered. "And what dead woman would that be?"

"Tara Warner," Sheldon replied without a trace of guile. "She told me right before I killed her. She told me you had seen her death, and that's why you appeared on the street that night. She said you would solve everything and avenge her."

"You still raped and killed her anyway, didn't you?"

"I didn't mean to," Sheldon said. "I just couldn't help myself. It's a compulsion."

"Then you should get help."

"I did get help," Sheldon said. "I was on medication for years. It curbed certain ... appetites. It also left me without my manly drive."

"You mean you couldn't get it up," Maddie said.

"There's no reason to be crude," Sheldon chided.

"Oh, no, we wouldn't want that," Maddie said. "You raped and murdered an innocent woman, but me being crude is the real crime."

"Tara wasn't my first ... friend," Sheldon said. "She was the first in a long while, though. Once I saw her, I knew I didn't want to be neutered any longer. I did fight it. I fought it for a long time. Then ... well ... I just decided I wanted to be me."

Sheldon moved a few feet into the room. Maddie refused to back up, or show fear.

"Do you know what the greatest crime is?" Sheldon asked. "It's not rape, or murder, or even genocide. It's trying to change who you are. I wanted to be a better man, and I was for a time. I don't want to be a better man any longer, though. I want to be the man I was born to be."

"Is that your excuse?" Maddie asked. "You're just trying to be you?"

"If it's any consolation, you're not even my type," Sheldon said. "I prefer a more ... delicate woman. You're too tall, and I'm not fond of blondes. I have no sexual interest in you. I won't rape you, Maddie."

"Well, thanks for the update."

"I have to kill you, though," Sheldon said. "You're the one person in this town who can ruin things for me. I have to quiet you. I don't have a choice."

"Don't take another step in this direction," Maddie said. "You'll regret it if you do."

Sheldon snorted as he advanced. "How do you figure that?"

Maddie was out of options. She drew her hand out of the drawer and slashed out in a wide, arcing motion, catching Sheldon dead center on his chest and causing him to cry out. Maddie slashed one more time for good measure, and then she bolted out of the kitchen and escaped into the bowels of the house.

"IT'S GOT TO BE HIM," Kreskin said, pointing at the screen. "He was living in the area where the women in Detroit were raped. He was less than a mile from each crime scene."

"It's too much of a coincidence," Nick agreed. "Now we have to find him."

"What are we going to do then?" Kreskin asked.

"We're going to question him," Nick said. "We'll compel him to take a DNA test."

"That's easier said than done," Kreskin said. "If Higgins is smart, he'll just lawyer up. We don't have enough evidence to force him to take a DNA test."

"So, what do you suggest?"

"We follow him until we can get a sample of his DNA to run on our own," Kreskin said. "Anything he discards, be it gum, or a water bottle, or a pop can, we can gather all of that once he discards it. We can legally run that."

"That could take too long," Nick protested.

"Then we'll have to take shifts watching him," Kreskin said. "It might take a few days, but it's our best option."

Nick knew he was speaking the truth, but he was frustrated. That's when he heard whispering in his ear. He cocked his head to the side and listened. He couldn't see her, but he could hear Olivia's voice. It was weak, and she was pleading with him.

Nick snapped to attention. "We have to get over to Maddie's."

"Why?" Kreskin was surprised by his outburst.

"She's in trouble." Nick was already striding toward the door.

"How do you know that?"

"I just do. Come on."

MADDIE RACED through the dark hallway at the back of the house, pushing her way into the garage and looking around. The vehicle door was down, and since Maude and Maddie never parked their cars inside, it was more of a catchall of family junk than anything else now. The door wasn't even electric. You had to pull it up manually.

"Oh, don't run, Maddie," Sheldon called after her. "You're just going to make it harder on yourself."

Maddie ignored him and scanned the garage for a weapon, her gaze landing on an old baseball bat. Maddie recognized it. It was Nick's. He'd given it to her after he'd hit a walk-off grand slam in the district championship game their senior year. He'd autographed it as a joke, but she'd kept it anyway. It was a part of him. It was a part of them.

Maddie tucked the knife into the pocket of her jeans, being careful not to catch her hand on it as she moved, and then wrapped her hand around the bat. The knife was deadlier, but the bat would allow Maddie to keep more distance between herself and Sheldon – and what she needed right now was distance.

"There you are," Sheldon said, appearing in the doorway. His shirt was shredded in the front, and blood was pooling in the open wound. It wasn't deep, but it was nasty enough to need stitches. "You took me by surprise back there, Maddie. Good for you. It will make your passing easier if you put up a fight."

"Thanks for the tip."

"What do you have in your hand now? Is that a baseball bat? Forgive me, I didn't realize you were a sports enthusiast."

"My interests are varied," Maddie said. "This isn't my bat, though. It's Nick's. He gave it to me a long time ago."

"For protection?"

"For love."

"Oh, you two are so sweet," Sheldon said. "I really am sorry that I'm going to have to end your love affair before you get a chance to explore it. If it weren't for your gifts, you wouldn't even be on my radar, Maddie."

"Stay over there," Maddie ordered, gesturing emphatically with the bat.

"Do you think you can take me?"

"You wouldn't be the first madman to underestimate me," Maddie said. "Just ask Todd Winthrop and Dustin Bishop."

"I was under the impression that Nick took them down."

"We did it as a team."

"You're just making this harder on yourself, Maddie," Sheldon said. "You understand that, right? I had no intention of scaring you. I was going to come back from the bathroom and take you by surprise from behind. It would have been quick. You wouldn't have felt fear."

"It's too late for that."

"How did you know?"

Maddie shrugged. "A little birdie told me."

"A ghost?"

Maddie didn't move or answer.

"Was it Tara's ghost? Is she still hanging around?"

"Would you care if she was?" Maddie asked. "Would that prey on you?"

"I don't like the idea of anyone suffering," Sheldon said. "I really am a good man."

"A good man doesn't rape women. A good man doesn't murder them."

"You don't understand," Sheldon said. "I am a good man. I just can't control my impulses. It's not my fault. I was born this way."

"That's the defense of a sociopath."

"And who's to say they're not right?"

"Anyone who isn't crazy," Maddie snapped.

"You're really starting to get tiresome, Maddie," Sheldon said. "You're not even trying to understand my side in all of this."

"I guess I'm just bitchy like that," Maddie deadpanned.

"I don't want to be a monster," Sheldon said. "I just *am* a monster. I tried to fight it, but I'm tired. Don't I deserve a little bit of relief?"

"Sure. As long as you don't hurt anyone else in the process."

"Well, that's not how my particular situation works," Sheldon said. "I wish I had other options, but I don't. You know, when this first started, I didn't kill. I let myself into the homes of the women I found desirable, I spent a few hours with them, and then I left them with their lives.

"I still watched them, though," he continued. "I couldn't help myself. I watched them struggle. I watched them cry. I watched them fall into alcoholism and drug abuse. I watched two of them kill themselves.

"Ask yourself an important question, Maddie," he said. "Is it better to let them linger and suffer, or is it better to snuff out the darkness before it consumes them? If you ask me, I did Tara a service. She didn't have to dwell on what I did. She was happy right before I took her. That has to count for something."

"You're crazy," Maddie spat. "You stay over there!"

"I'm going to be honest with you," Sheldon said. "I'm running out of time. I have no idea when Nick will return. He's been glued to your side lately. I was watching you at the fireworks the other night, and I thought I'd have a chance then. Unfortunately, Ms. Ford was your shadow that evening until Nick returned.

"Don't worry, though," he said. "I think Ms. Ford and I are going to have a good time once you're gone. She's going to need a shoulder to cry on."

"Don't you dare touch her," Maddie threatened, waving the bat in his face. "I'll kill you."

"How can you kill me if you're already dead?" Sheldon took a step forward. "I'm going to have to end this now. I don't have a lot of options. I'll make sure to give Nick extra time off to mourn you. Who knows? When it's all said and done, when he's done grieving, maybe he'll give Cassidy another shot. If he can't have his great love, maybe the woman who loves him greatly will be enough."

Sheldon lunged for her, but Maddie was ready. She gripped the bat with both hands and swung. Hard. When the bat connected with the side of Sheldon's face, he looked momentarily surprised.

The sound of wood hitting bone was unmistakable, and Sheldon grunted upon impact. He tried to remain standing, but he was losing consciousness. Just as he hit the floor, the garage door flew open.

Maddie turned swiftly, prepared to fight off a second assailant if need be. Instead of death, though, Maddie came face to face with love as Nick stormed into the garage with Kreskin on his heels.

"Maddie?" Nick grabbed her, pulling her to him as Kreskin moved over to Sheldon and drew his gun.

"Nicky," Maddie said, wrapping her arms around his neck. "Nicky."

"I thought ... I thought we were going to be too late." Nick was crying. "I thought I was going to lose you."

"You'll never lose me, Nicky," Maddie said, kissing his cheek. "You'll never lose me. Not again. I promise."

26. TWENTY-SIX

Nick found Maddie asleep on the window seat a few hours later. She'd answered questions for hours, and then asked a few of her own. While the crime techs were working, she'd disappeared into the house to rest. Nick had checked on her periodically, but he gave her the space she needed to process. He didn't want to crowd her – or smother her.

While the paramedics said that Sheldon would survive, Nick wasn't sure how he felt about it. Part of him was glad Maddie hadn't killed him because it would be hard for her to deal with on an emotional level. The other part of him didn't want a piece of filth like Sheldon to go on living.

Nick shifted Maddie over slightly and climbed up on the window seat with her. Maddie instinctively reached for him, even though she didn't wake up. Nick pulled her head onto his chest and kissed the top of her head.

That's where Kreskin found them five minutes later. "The garage is clear. I made sure all the blood was cleaned up."

"You didn't have to do that," Nick said. "I could have done it tomorrow."

"I think you guys have dealt with enough," Kreskin said. "It really wasn't that bad. His shirt absorbed most of it. Do you want me to help you get her upstairs?"

Nick shook his head. "We can sleep here."

"Isn't that a little tight for you?"

"We've been sleeping here for years," he said. "We make it work. Olivia built it for us so we had a place to hang out when she was working in the shop. It's Maddie's favorite place in the house."

"Which means it's your favorite place in the house," Kreskin finished.

"Pretty much."

"Is that who told you to go looking for Maddie tonight?" Kreskin asked.

Nick stilled. "What do you mean?"

"Right before you bolted out of the police station, you looked like you were listening to someone."

"I wasn't." Nick felt panic well in his chest.

"You know there are rumors about Maddie, right?"

"I don't care."

"I'm just telling you that I know what's going on here," Kreskin said. "Olivia was known as a fake psychic, and yet people believed she was a real psychic. I'm guessing her daughter has the same gifts, which would explain why she ran as a teenager. Olivia came to you tonight, didn't she? Only a mother could be strong enough to make you listen."

"I don't know what you're talking about."

Kreskin pursed his lips. "You don't have to tell me. I understand why you're keeping it secret. Look at it this way, you learned a valuable lesson today."

"And what lesson was that?"

"Maddie took care of herself," Kreskin said. "In the end, she didn't need you to rescue her."

"She's strong," Nick said, rubbing the back of her head as she slumbered.

"She is. You are, too. You're strong together. Now, why don't you get some sleep together? You look exhausted."

Kreskin moved toward the door. "Oh, you can have tomorrow off. It should be a slow day, and I'm betting you'd rather play kissy-face with her than work."

"I'd always rather do that," Nick said, grinning. "Thanks."

"You've earned it. Do you want me to lock the door on the way out?"

"Maude will do it when she comes in."

"Where is Maude?" Kreskin asked, looking around.

"I have no idea," Nick said, rubbing his forehead. "She's probably out stalking Harriet Proctor."

"Do you want me to find her?"

"No. She'll come home when she's good and ready."

"Are you going to yell at her about the cup?"

"No," Nick said. "Speaking of that, though, what are we going to do about Charles Harper?"

"I'll pick him up tomorrow. Don't worry about it."

"You're a good guy," Nick said.

"So are you. Take care of your girl."

"Always."

MADDIE woke an hour later to find Nick watching her sleep. "Hi."

"Hi, love."

"Why didn't you wake me up?"

"How many times do I have to tell you, it's a crime to wake a sleeping angel."

Maddie smiled. "Are you hungry?"

"Not really," Nick said. "You scared the hunger right out of me."

"How did you know?"

"Your mother came to me. She was weak, but I could still hear her."

"She's the one who warned me," Maddie said. "Sheldon said he was going to sneak up behind me and kill me, but Mom warned me so I wasn't where he expected to find me. She saved me."

"Even in death, Olivia is watching out for us," Nick said. He kissed Maddie softly. "Do you want to go up to bed?"

"Are you tired?"

"I'm ... exhausted, but I'm not sure I'm ready to sleep yet."

Maddie smiled. "Good. I have an idea."

Nick arched an eyebrow. "What idea?"

"Trust me."

"I CAN'T BELIEVE you want to do this," Nick said, staring out at the placid water and smiling. When Maddie had suggested taking a walk to Willow Lake, Nick thought it was merely because she wanted to unwind. She had something else in mind, though.

"Why not? Don't you want to?"

Nick smirked. "Maddie, just for the record, I always want to go skinny dipping with you. If it's thirty degrees and freezing, if you're going to be naked, I'm there. I just never thought you would be the one to suggest it."

Maddie whipped her tank top off, revealing a pretty lace bra, and focused on him. "It's come to my attention that I might be a little too timid."

"You're not timid, you're cautious." Nick found he could barely drag his eyes away from Maddie's bra. "You know, I'm standing by my moratorium. We're not doing it tonight. We're both tired, and you've had a horrible day. I'm not marking one of the worst days of my life with something I've been dreaming about for a decade."

"Who said anything about sex?" Maddie asked, unsnapping her jean shorts and letting them drop to the ground.

Nick almost growled when he saw her matching panties. Her body was a marvel. Her legs were long and lean, and her hips were narrow. Her abdomen was flat and defined, and her breasts were perfectly formed without being too large. He'd never seen anything more lovely.

"Can't we just ... swim?"

"Yes," Nick said, automatically reaching for his shirt and stripping it off. He dropped his shorts a second later and then waited, cocking an eyebrow in challenge. "Do you want me to go first, or are you going to go first?"

Maddie smiled. She didn't say a word as she unfastened her bra and tossed it on the ground. She was silent when she pulled her panties down. The only sound Nick could hear was the beating of his own heart.

Maddie leaned over and kissed him, and then she turned and raced into the water – giggling like a madwoman as she ran. Nick watched her, love filling his heart. After a moment, he stripped off his boxers and followed.

He finally had everything he ever wanted, and now he was going to enjoy it. Nothing would ever separate them again.

Made in United States
Troutdale, OR
10/29/2023